A World of Their Own

a novel by

Frank Allan Rogers

ISBN 13:978-1-951543-23-5 —Print
ISBN 13: 978-1-951543-24-2 —eBook

Frank Allan Rogers 2023

Printed in
The United States of America

Dedication

This book is dedicated to Curtis Rogers. I sincerely appreciate all the comments, suggestions, and critiques. Thank you, brother.

Acknowledgements

I try always to make my fiction stories authentic. My readers deserve that. But I could never do it alone, and I truly appreciate those who help.

To my beta readers who always improve the quality of my writing. You are more important than you know.

> Debra Watzman
> Judy Moody
> Mark Warr
> Sandra Warr

For the Carrollton Writers Guild, a tremendous group of authors always eager to help another author polish a manuscript.

A special thanks to my darling wife, Mary – for your encouragement, understanding, and patience while I write. And for your honesty when you read those occasional paragraphs for me to see if they made sense – some yes, some no. I couldn't do it without you.

Chapter One

Propped up on his elbow, the man in the bed by the window cleared his throat and spoke out loud.

"It's gonna be another great day. Maybe I'll see a beautiful smile, make a new friend, or find a great book to read."

The man on the bed by the door yanked the chain and screamed at the handcuff that tortured his wrist. He sat up and yelled across the room.

"Hey, you old fool, don't you ever shut up? You been talking to yourself for two days straight."

The man by the window grunted. "I can't lay on a hospital bed for a week without talking to somebody."

"You ain't been here a week. I was here three days before you."

"I'll be here a few more days, and I talk to myself because *you* don't talk."

"You hear me talking sometimes. I *know* you do."

"You mean when you yell at your handcuffs? That's a *great* conversation."

"Whaddaya think, old man? If you'd been shot in the butt and chained to the bed, would *you* be okay?"

"Maybe not. But I try to look at the better side of things. I've been in other hospitals. This one's better."

"Better for *you*. You ain't headed for the slammer when you get out of here. If so, you'd be chained up like me. So, what wonderful things do you see in my life?"

"I watched when you went down the hall with the nurse yesterday. You walked much better."

"Yeah, the faster my hip heals, the sooner I go to trial."

"Trial? You said you're headed for prison."

"My court-appointed lawyer and the county prosecutor … they're not friends of mine." He held up crossed fingers. "But they've been friends with each other for a long time. I know them, and I know how it'll turn out."

"I've heard the doctor and nurses call you Hardy. That's your last name?"

"It's my first name."

"I'm Seth."

Without knocking, the officer on duty pushed open the door and walked in, followed by a nurse.

"I'm Rosie," she announced with a huge grin. "You need the restroom before your walk?"

Hardy stared. "No, but I'd like to put on some pants."

"You'll have to wear the gown as long as you're here."

The officer took a key from his pocket, unhooked the handcuff from the bed, fastened it to Hardy's free wrist, and removed the cuff from his ankle.

Dipping his head at his bare knees, Hardy grumbled and turned to the nurse. "I'm six feet and two inches tall. This gown's way too short."

The nurse motioned at the gown while the three walked out of the room. "I know. What we say here is, *one size fits none.*"

Seth rolled on his side with his back toward the other bed and pulled the sheet past his eyes. He'd like to grab a nap before his roommate returned. An hour later, Seth jerked awake and rolled over when he heard, "Ahhh, I hate this."

"You okay?"

"Whadda you care, old man?"

"My name is Seth."

"Okay, why should I care about your name? Any way you can help me?"

"How did your walk go today?"

"Fine. Better than yesterday. But can you help me?"

"Maybe in the near future. But you must be open-minded, willing to cooperate, and believe."

"Oh, BS." Hardy lay back on the bed. Then he sat up, drank water, belched, and cleared his throat. "Believe what?"

Seth sat up. "I can take you out of here to a place you've never been."

"More BS. You have no idea where I've been."

"No, but I do know a place you've never been ,,, never heard of. I can take you there only if you trust me and do everything I ask until you get there."

Hardy laughed. "Yeah? And then what? Some kind of miracle?"

"You'll have a whole new life. Make new friends. But chances are, you'll never again see anyone you know here except me."

Hardy offered a huge grin with an exaggerated nod. "I can't wait. Any unicorns?"

Seth lay back on his bed and picked up his book.

Hardy lay back on his own bed and mumbled. After a minute of dead silence, he sat up and rattled his chains.

"You're freakin' me out, old man. Sounds like a fairytale."

Seth did not sit up or take his eyes off the book. "The name's Seth." *Why did I offer to help that guy? He's a real jerk.*

The next morning, Seth napped after breakfast but woke to the sound of voices on the other side of the heavy vinyl curtain which separated the room.

"Well, Mister Brooke, it's *your* decision. I'm not saying you should plead guilty to the current charges. I'm your attorney. I'm suggesting an option. You have no prior record. If you plead guilty to a lesser charge, you will likely get a lighter sentence, maybe one year in jail."

"*Only one*? That woman across the street from me has never liked me. I don't care. She's crazy anyway. But, when I walked out of the grocery store that day, I saw her red car hightailing it out of the parking lot. When I got to my car, I had a big dent and red paint scuffs on my front fender."

"Did you call the police?"

"What for? I knew who did it. So, I drove to her house to talk to her, and she lied about everything. I asked her to open the garage and let me see her car. She told me to get the hell out of her house.

So… Nancy *Napalm* Naples started the whole thing. I'm the one who got shot, and I'm the one charged with a crime. Can you explain that Mister Attorney? I told you all of this before. I guess you forgot."

"You were in Nancy Naples' home without her consent. When you threatened her, she grabbed her gun from the drawer. You spun around and…lucky for you…the bullet hit your backside."

"What? You and the prosecutor just took her word for all that happened?"

"No, no. Miss Naples has security cameras inside and outside her home. The prosecutor has a copy of everything. We watched it yesterday at his office. Before she shot you, we saw you hold up your hands like you were choking somebody, and you screamed that you would get even."

Hardy gave a heavy sigh. "You can't believe I would've hurt her? I've never choked anybody or hit a woman in my life."

The attorney's voice came clear and strong above the snapping and zipping sounds of a closing briefcase. "What I believe has no bearing on this case. If this goes to court, the jury will see everything I saw. Can I convince them it was all her fault? Or that you were not serious? Or it never happened? The jury would likely consider the lady homeowner acted in self-defense and the intruder committed a crime. That's what you're looking at, young man. Here's my card. Call my office by tomorrow afternoon and give me your decision, please, so I can get everything prepared."

The door opened. Feet shuffled. The door closed.

An officer waited by the door while an attendant came in and pushed open the big curtain. The attendant looked at each man. "Either of you need anything?"

After his fake laugh, Hardy glanced at the officer, back to the attendant, and held up his cuffed hand. "I need a key."

"Sorry, buddy, that's the one thing I can't bring you." He nodded at the water cup. "Need more water?"

Hardy lowered his head and glared. "What for? So I can drown myself?"

The attendant looked up at the ceiling as he and the officer walked out and shut the door.

Seth sat up, swung his feet off the bed and onto the floor. "Good morning, Hardy."

Hardy smirked. "You know something I don't? Where's the good part?"

"Sorry to bother you." Seth picked a book off the bedside table and rested his head on his pillow. "I won't do it again."

Minutes later, Hardy sat up and leaned over. "Hey, Seth, sorry about all that. I may be totally out of my mind, but I got nothin' to lose. Your offer, whatever it is, sounds better than a year in jail. That is …if the offer still stands."

Seth left his bed and sat in a guest chair near his roommate. "Since you called me by my name, we can discuss it. But if…and *only if*…you make a solemn commitment. So pay attention to what I say. Also, there's a lot I have to leave out, but if I decide to help you, you'll learn a lot more in a few days."

Hardy sat on the edge of his bed, and leaned forward, his eyes focused on Seth. "Okay, what do you need to know?"

Seth wiped his brow and folded his hands. "A few things I need to ask to see if you're a good fit for a complete change in your life."

"Okay. Go."

"You live here in Ohio?"

"Yep. Born right here in Lorain twenty-two years ago. I still live here."

"You married?"

"I almost made that mistake a couple of years ago, but no."

"Any kids?"

Hardy chuckled and shook his head. "No. Been lucky, I guess."

"Family?"

"Sort of. An uncle and aunt in Cleveland. Haven't seen 'em since my parents' funeral. I'm an only child. I live in my parents' house, the one they left me."

Seth cleared his throat. "Your parents are deceased?"

Hardy turned, breathed deep, and looked at Seth. "Back in … two-thousand-one … my grandparents took a vacation to New York. They were in one of the Trade Towers when it came down." He rubbed his hand across his eyes. "Two years ago, my parents drove out to the cemetery here in Lorain to visit the graves. On their way home, a drunk driver killed 'em both." He paused. "My parents are buried next to my grandparents. I've never been to the cemetery to visit their graves." He shook his head. "And I never will."

Hardy took deep breaths, spread his hands, and turned to Seth. "That stuff is tough to talk about. Is that all you need?"

Seth rubbed the lump in his throat. "That's all. But there are a couple of things I need to tell you. This journey involves a train trip, and there's no turning back once you're on the train. Not ever. It's the decision of a lifetime because it's a lifetime commitment. Think about that for a couple of minutes."

"Can't we drive? I have a car."

"No cars. Are you willing to go along with everything I tell you? There's no other way to do this. Are you ready? Yes? Or no?"

Hardy's eyes grew big. "If I decide to do this, when will it happen? Before I go to jail?"

Seth's face showed no expression. "Tomorrow."

"Are you serious? How about a couple days? I wanna think about it for a day or two."

"Can't do that," Seth replied. "I'll be out of here tomorrow. At my age … no time to wait."

Hardy sat up straight. "Pardon me, but everything you say seems weirder than before. How old *are* you?"

"Tomorrow's my birthday. I'll be one hundred."

Hardy's sarcastic laugh filled the room until he covered his face. "You're putting me on. You might look old, but you don't look *that* old." After another short laugh, he looked up. "Sorry, man, you had me convinced for a while. But now …." He stabbed a button on the monitor. "I gotta get somebody in here for a couple of minutes." He nodded toward the restroom. "And then, I gotta hit the sack. I'm beat."

After the officer and attendant came and left, Seth rose from his chair and stood by the young man's bed. "Just so you know, everything I said tonight is true. *Everything*. I wouldn't joke about anything that important."

Hardy stared at the ceiling. "What is it that makes your dream world so special? What kind of people live there?" He looked at Seth.

"Ordinary people just like you. But the people of Mystique are rarely influenced by people from distant cultures and time periods. They have every reason to be happy, and they are. They live in a world of their own."

Hardy lay back on his bed. "A world of their own." He smiled, closed his eyes, and repeated, "A world of their own."

In his bed, Seth shrugged, picked up his book, and dropped it once more on the table. He turned off the reading light and climbed into bed.

In an hour or so, Seth stirred, groggy, while a noise tried to invade his sleep. Irritated, he pushed it from his mind and floated into blissful peace once more.

It came again, a voice that seemed a mile away. *Was it real or an aggravating dream?*

"Seth, you awake?"

Seth groaned and sat up. He rubbed his face. "Hardy … is that you?"

"Yeah, man, we're the only people in the room."

Seth sighed. "Why are you bothering me?"

"I can't come over there. Can you come over here for a minute? I gotta tell you something."

Seth slouched to the other bed and stood with his hands folded.

"Listen, Seth. I went to sleep thinking of what you said about a new life. It woke me up, and I have to try it. So, I'm saying yes to your offer. I want out of here tomorrow. I'll do whatever you say, but you'd better not let me down."

"My word is a solemn bond. See you tomorrow."

"Wait. Anything else you need to tell me?"

Seth nodded. "A lot. But not now."

"Happy birthday, Seth … in case you don't make it till morning." Hardy laughed.

***

Whispers jerked Hardy awake. He rubbed his eyes. The big wall clock showed 6:07 AM. *There should be more light in the room unless it's raining.* He turned to look out the window but saw nothing but the huge vinyl curtain that divided the room.

His heart fluttered. *Seth must be up to something. Today, he turns one hundred, and I get to leave this miserable place.*

He trembled with excitement. Sweat broke out on his face. He sat up but lay back again when the curtain opened. Two men pushed a gurney toward the door.

Hardy sat up straight again and gasped. The top sheet on the gurney … it covered … a body. The men rolled the gurney from the room and closed the door.

Hardy covered his face. His chin quivered. "Oh, my God."

Chapter Two

A good-looking orderly wheeled her food cart into the room behind the officer. Hardy drew a ragged breath, wiped his bloodshot eyes on the sheet, and sat up.

She smiled. "Good morning. You slept well, I hope?"

He covered his eyes. "No."

She dipped her head toward him. "Hungry?"

"I need something for a headache. Got any aspirin?"

She placed the tray of food on his bed table and swung the table in front of him. "No, but I have fresh orange juice for you this morning. I hope you're hungry."

Hardy dragged his hand off his face and stared up at her. "You know anything about the patient who was in here last night?" He angled his head toward the other side of the room. "He was an old guy, and he talked a lot."

"I'm sorry, Mister…" she glanced at the patient info on the foot of the bed. "Mister Brooke. I have no information about other patients. Enjoy your breakfast. Let me know if you need anything."

"I got a headache. I *need* some aspirin." He wanted to say, wait a minute as she and the officer walked out. He needed to hear about Seth." But he knew it would be pointless.

Hardy ate little. He pushed the bed table aside, lay back, and pulled the sheet over his face. But when his mind saw a sudden image of Seth under that sheet, Hardy yanked the sheet from his face.

So much for relying on Seth. I should've known from the start that he's a phony. And I guess that makes me a total idiot for buying his crazy tale.

What am I going to do now? What am I going to do when I get out of here? What am I going to do with the rest of my life?

Oh no… this means I gotta go through a trial. And who knows what will happen then? Or I'll have to plead guilty to something.

I can never tell anybody about this day or about that old man. They'll think I'm as nutty as he was. Good thing for him I'll never see him again. I'd get even.

After two hours of sleep, Hardy sat up and rubbed his face. In place of the breakfast tray, he found a cup of fresh water. Next to the water, an aspirin. Next to the aspirin, his attorney's calling card. He did not remember putting it there, but strange things had happened in the last few hours.

He downed the aspirin with a big gulp of water, picked up the card, and the phone. *May as well get it over with.*

A pleasant voice answered. "Good morning, Attorney Graham's office."

"This is Hardy Brooke. I need to speak with my attorney, please." The discussion took just five minutes. The attorney would come to the hospital the next day for signatures.

Hardy breathed a sigh of relief. *Maybe the best thing is to take my chances. If it means a year in jail, it will be the hardest thing I've ever done in my life. But I can survive.*

After lunch, he tried everything he could to teach himself to be a positive thinker but made little progress. Serving a year in prison would have an awful effect on his life forever, even if he lived to be a hundred. He chuckled at the thought, but his chest tightened as tears filled his eyes.

TV had never been his favorite pastime. But after dinner, he turned it on, hoping it would distract him from all the bad news in his own life. But the bad news on TV made everything worse. *What was left to live for?* Exhausted, he switched off the TV and lay back on the bed.

Hours passed. A slight noise outside his room brought Hardy almost awake. Something bumped his bed.

Hardy sat up, eyes wide, breathing heavily. "Hey, what's going on? Who are you? Get out of my room, or I'll …."

"Hardy, get up. It's time to go. And don't turn on any lights."

"What? Seth … Seth, is that you? Oh, my God. I thought you …"

"It's me. Come on, Hardy. Work with me. We have to be at the train station before midnight." Seth grabbed a key from his pocket and opened the cuffs. "Get up. Get out of that gown. Here." He threw a handful of clothes on the bed. "Put these on."

"But, Seth, my clothes …"

"Forget 'em. Put these on, and hurry. No time for questions."

Three minutes later, his eyes scanned Hardy. "Okay." He grabbed Hardy's shoulders, pulled him forward, and plopped a hat on his head.

"Now, young man, we're gonna walk out of here … *fast*. Stay beside me, and don't talk to anyone but me. Answer my questions. Nothing else. Oh…and try not to limp."

The wall clock showed 11:00 PM when Seth opened the door. Hardy glanced in the mirror on his way out. His mouth fell open. Both men wore police uniforms.

Behind a desk in the hallway, a woman yelled, "Excuse me."

Hardy slowed. Seth spoke in a loud whisper. "Walk fast. Don't turn around." Quick footsteps from behind gained on them. Seth whispered again. "Keep going. Hurry to the elevator. Wait for me in the taxi parked out front. Don't talk to anybody but the driver."

"Excuse me, Mister Police Officer."

Seth stopped and turned. "Sorry, Ma'am. An emergency call just came in. You can see it on TV news." Seth whirled and started away.

From behind, he heard, "Oh, my. Sorry. Be careful, please." He did not reply as he hurried to the elevator.

The elevator door opened on the ground floor, where a police officer waited to get on. Seth's heart caught in his throat. "Hello, uh …" he glanced at the man's name tag.

"Lieutenant Winston. A nurse is waiting for you on floor five."

The lieutenant's forehead wrinkled. "For me? What for?"

Seth shrugged. "Didn't say but seemed in a hurry to see you. Sorry, I don't know her name." He sprinted for the exit and called over his shoulder. "Floor five."

Relieved to find Hardy in the back seat of Charlie's Cab, Seth sat in the front seat and pointed at the instrument panel. "Is that clock right? 11:07?"

Charlie nodded, "Dead on."

"Take us to Benson Road, Charlie. I'll give you directions to the train station from there."

The driver shook his head. "Sorry, there's no train station in that direction. Nothin' but junkyards and warehouses. And … a few houses of ill repute. Know what I mean?"

"Trust me, Charlie. I know you've never seen the station, but it's there." Seth pulled money from his pocket and flashed a hundred-dollar bill. "Here's your tip if you follow my directions and get us there on time."

Taxi tires squealed as Charlie headed for the highway. "I'll take you where you say, but I've been down Benson Road a hundred times and never seen a train station. Not even tracks."

"This time, you'll see both." Seth waved the money. "I'm betting a hundred bucks on it."

Charlie shrugged again. "If we turn right on Benson, it leads to Charleston. No train station between here and the next town."

Seth nodded. "I know. Turn left on Benson."

"Left?" Charlie's voice rose. "That's a dead-end."

Seth smiled. "I'll show you when we arrive." He pulled another hundred from his pocket and waved them at the cabbie. Both of these are yours if you drive where I tell you and if you get us to the station before midnight. It's about another fifty-five miles. No time to waste."

Seth turned to look at Hardy. "You have not uttered a word since we left the parking lot. You all right? How's your uhh … injury?"

"It's okay. But I'm confused. Been around this area all my life, and on Benson many times, but never seen a train station anywhere."

Seth smiled. "It'll be okay." He pointed at the seat beside Hardy. "You see a suitcase I left there?"

"Yeah. I moved it to the floor."

"Okay. Grab it when we get out. We'll need that before we can board the train."

They fell silent for a few minutes while the driver shook his head at every street sign. Seth watched the clock and *nodded* at every street sign. The driver pointed at a sign. "Benson Road. 8 Miles."

Seth glanced at the clock again. "Okay, Charlie. Make a left onto Benson. I'll give you directions after that. Whatever you do, don't slow down."

"I been going over the speed limit since we left the hospital. Any faster … we may get stopped by the police. That's the last thing *I* need. And you too."

"Good point, Charlie. Remember we have to be inside that station before it closes at midnight."

"Yeah, well, if you show me train tracks on Benson Road, I'll get you there on time. If you can't, I still get the money, right?"

Seth held out his hands and shrugged. "That won't be a problem."

The cab grew quiet until Seth pointed at another sign. *Benson Road, One Mile.*

Charlie nodded. "I see the sign." Yet, he stopped the car on the side of the road and pointed to a new sign. No Left Turn. Road Closed.

Chapter Three

Seth sat up straight. "We're going to turn left anyway, Charlie. You gotta get back on the road. Please do what I ask. Everything will be fine."

Hardy rested his hand on top of Seth's seatback. "Hey, Seth, I have to butt in. You must be confused about all this."

"I'm not confused. I am on a mission, and we have to do everything the way I say, or it will not work. We can still get there on time if everybody cooperates. Do you want to go to jail again? If you don't, you have to believe in me."

Hardy grabbed the back of the seat again. "I'll do whatever you say. I'm out of options."

Seth pulled another hundred-dollar bill from his pocket and waved it at Charlie. "This will also be yours if you do what I asked. So … last chance. If you stall any longer, we may not arrive on time, and you won't get paid."

Charlie shrugged and drove onto the road without speaking. When he tried to turn left on Benson, he stopped and pointed. "You see that roadblock."

Seth chuckled. "It's a big, plastic sawhorse." He jumped from the car and moved the sawhorse aside. After Charlie made the turn, Seth replaced the roadblock and scrambled into the car. "Okay, Charlie, the horse is back in the corral. Full speed ahead."

The driver started forward.

"Trust me," Seth told him. He glanced at the clock again. "Everything's going to be fine if we keep moving as fast as we can."

After they passed all businesses on Benson, a huge sign in front of them read Dead End.

"Drive around," Seth yelled, "and keep going."

Charlie jerked his head. "Whatta you mean? Can't you see what's behind that sign? It's nothing but a field of weeds. I can't drive through that."

"Trust me, Charlie. Just trust me. That will take us where we need to go."

"Wait a minute. You said nothing about this. You expect me to drive my cab across that?"

"We are running out of time, Charlie. You will get no money from me if you stop now. Do you understand?"

Charlie drew a deep breath and drove around the sign into the weeds. "Okay, but I gotta tell you, I feel foolish doing this. You're gonna have to pay me no matter what happens."

"Just keep going, Charlie, and you will earn your fare … and your tip."

Hardy leaned forward. "Okay, *I* gotta tell you, Seth, I'm starting to agree with our driver. Looks like I'm going to wind up in jail. And you could wind up in the asylum."

Seth did not turn around. "Stick with me, Hardy. I have not steered you wrong, and I won't."

The cab slipped left to right and snaked through the giant weeds. Charlie's head turned side-to-side, keeping time with the car. Sweat beaded on his cheeks and his neck. "Aww, man, I don't believe this. These weeds are taller than the car. I'd hate to get stuck out here in the middle of nowhere. I bet getting my cab out of this mess would cost me three hundred dollars."

The car slid sideways and stopped. The wheels spun. The car would not move. Charlie pulled a big red bandanna from the pouch next to him. He wiped his face and hair, replaced the bandanna, and turned to Seth. "Okay, this is exactly what I was afraid of. So … no offense … but what's your new plan, *Money Man?*"

"Stay where you are, Charlie." Seth stepped out into the mud and yelled, "Follow me." He walked through the least muddy areas. Charlie followed and steered the cab to almost dry land.

"I think we should be okay now," Seth offered.

Charlie's head made a slow wag. He did not speak.

"We lost valuable time," Seth reminded as he glanced at the clock. "Keep her going, Charlie. We should be out of this mess any time."

Charlie's face showed defeat. He glanced at Seth but did not speak while the car pushed down the weeds.

Hardy leaned forward. "I gotta tell you, Seth. This is the craziest mess I've ever seen. I don't know where we are and have no idea where we're trying to go. But I don't have much faith in this so-called *mission*. Sorry, it ain't working."

Seth looked at the clock again. "We have about forty-two minutes. We can still make it … with no further problems."

With a heavy sigh, Charlie turned to Seth. "I can't believe this. We don't know where we are or where we're going. So how could you think we can get to some mystical place when nobody seems to know where it is or how far."

Seth smiled. "Oh, but I know where it is and how far. So, keep the faith."

"Faith? *What* faith? If you know where it is and *think* you know how far, how about telling *me*? I am the driver. Don't you think I need to know?"

Seth grinned. "I suppose you have a point. We've got about thirty-three minutes to get there and about forty-five miles to go."

"Oh, great. I have to drive 90 miles an hour. You know how long it will take to go that far in this stuff?" He dipped his head at the field of weeds.

Seth nodded. "All that will change very soon."

Charlie's face wrinkled. He turned to look at Seth. "I've never met anybody like you. I'll be eternally grateful if we ever get out of here alive. But I don't honestly believe what you're telling me."

Seth grinned again. "Okay, if you don't believe, take another look at what's ahead."

Charlie's head snapped around. "Oh, my God."

Hardy gasped. "*Oh my God,* is right. What is this?"

Seth grinned again. "Everybody happy now?"

His wide eyes staring ahead, Charlie sat up, bouncing in his seat. "I have never seen this highway. It looks new, and there's nobody on it. Just a beautiful, clean stretch of asphalt with white stripes on the edges. Now *this* I can drive on."

"I like to hear that." Seth stabbed his finger toward a sign. *Train 43 Miles.* "We have…" he glanced at the clock again… "33 minutes to get there. One minute late, and the train leaves without us."

For about five seconds, Charlie's eyes appeared almost closed. He looked at Seth. "So, I have to drive ninety miles an hour to get you there on time." He floored the gas pedal. "On this road, I can do that. I can do that and love it."

Seth turned to him. "Charlie, we won't have time to talk at the station. So, a couple of things I have to tell you. When you leave the station, don't try to come back in this direction. This road will not be here. I know that may sound impossible but trust me."

"Everything you do seems impossible to *me*," Charlie said.

"Yeah, I suppose it does. Remember, when you leave the station, keep turning right every time you can. You'll think you're going around in circles, but you will find a familiar road to take you home."

Charlie nodded. "That sounds pretty crazy, though I don't think it could get any crazier than this whole trip. But tell me what do I say to other people about this. Nobody will believe me. If somebody told *me*, I wouldn't believe it either."

Seth shrugged. "You won't have any problem with explaining it to anyone."

"What? How can you say that?"

"Once you get three miles from the station, your memory about all of this will begin to fade."

Charlie kept his eyes on the road. "Sorry, man, that's hard to believe. If I don't remember this road, I'll remember picking up you two at the hospital. And I'll never forget turning left on Benson Road and finding the road blocked. And I can't forget that big field of weeds, especially when I'm washing all the mud off my cab."

Seth grinned again. "You won't remember any of it, including the mud on your car. By the time you leave the station parking lot, the mud will be gone. Your tip will be the sole evidence you'll have of this trip. You won't remember how or why you have the tip, but it will be worth just as much."

Hardy leaned forward. "Well, Seth, does all that stuff apply to me? Will I forget everything about this trip and my entire past life? Will I remember any of the people I now know?

There's a lot you didn't explain. I might've made a different decision if you'd told me a lot more."

Seth turned and stared. "If I told you ahead of time about everything that's happened so far, you wouldn't be here. You thought I was crazy. Remember? Before you get on the train, you can still change your mind and ride home with Charlie. If you do that, you will wake up in handcuffs in your hospital bed, convinced the whole thing was one big, crazy dream."

"Oh, come on. From start to finish, this whole thing *seems* like a crazy dream. I don't know what life will be like in the world you're taking me to. You said it's a one-way trip. What if I hate it there?"

Seth shrugged. "No guarantees. No one can force you to be happy no matter where you are or who you're with. As I said before, you will find many reasons for a happy life in your new home. But … you can choose misery if that's what you want."

Charlie laughed. "I hate to butt in, guys." He pointed at a sign. "Train Station 12 Miles."

Seth looked at the clock again. "We made great time. Nine minutes left. But don't slow down."

Charlie's eyes grew wide. His mouth hung open. "Oh, no." He stabbed his finger at another sign. *Road Closed. 2 Miles Ahead.* Charlie tapped the brake.

Seth sat up straight. "Don't slow down, Charlie." He raised his voice. "Do not slow down."

Charlie scrunched his face. "But … I … don't …"

"Trust me, Charlie. Do *not* slow down."

Charlie pressed the gas pedal to the floor. His mouth dropped and he pointed straight ahead. "You see that big billboard in the middle of the road? It says *road closed*. I see no place to go around. If I keep going, it'll kill all of us."

22

Seth shouted, "Do not slow down, Charlie. Full speed ahead. Trust me on this one."

The cab crashed into the giant sign with thunderous, mingled noises of splintering wood, crunching steel, shattering glass, and screaming people.

Chapter Four

Five seconds after the car demolished the sign, silence ruled again while the undamaged cab streaked down the open road, while Charlie and Hardy struggled to catch their breath.

Seth chuckled. "Okay, guys, I apologize for this boring trip, but we're getting close."

Charlie glanced at him. "Boring? I would hate to go on a trip you call exciting."

With an uneasy laugh, Hardy leaned forward. "I don't think I could survive a trip scarier than this one."

Seth wore a big grin. "So … would either of you do it again?"

"What do you mean, again? Is there more stuff coming up?" Charlie's knuckles grew white on the steering wheel.

Seth shrugged. "Hard to tell on a trip like this. Know what I mean?"

"No. I *don't* know what you mean. There's no such thing as a *trip like this.*"

"You may be right." He pointed to another sign. *Train Station 3 Miles.*

Charlie frowned. "Yeah, well, I ain't believin' that. Seems like every time we see a sign, another blood-curdling disaster is about to scare the devil out of us. Maybe I should say a little prayer."

"Nothing wrong with that." Seth chuckled.

Hardy pointed ahead. "Hey, look. It's the train station, with lights all around."

"I think we're clear of the obstacles now, Charlie." Seth pointed to the station. "When you leave the station, turn right."

"Right? The station is on our *right*."

"Well, my friend if you turn left, you're gonna miss the road you need. Just follow what I say."

Charlie leaned forward. "All the lanterns are lit around the station, and I see some inside. But I don't see any cars. Looks like the station is closed."

"It's not closed. You won't see electric lights, but the lanterns inside are lit. That's the way it is. Turn right and cross the tracks when you get past the station."

"Okay," Charlie said. He slowed the cab to a crawl as they neared the station. "Wow, look at that. The train and the station look like they're two hundred years old, maybe more. The station house is made of logs, and that's a coal-burning steam engine. I've seen them in old cowboy movies, but I never thought I'd see one for real." He pulled the iPhone from the holster on his belt. "I gotta get some shots of all this. Nobody will believe me if I don't."

"Nobody's gonna believe anything. The shots won't turn out." Seth said.

Hardy leaned forward. "I don't know about all this. You think we should trust that old train?" His eyes narrowed. "You think that old thing will get us where you want to go? Besides, it looks like a rough ride if we ever get there."

Seth smiled. "I trust it more than any modern transportation. I've been on that train many times. It has never stalled and never been late."

Charlie stopped the cab and pointed. "You see that? The track stops at the tail end of the caboose."

Seth opened the door and stepped out. "We'll have to get out here, Charlie. We have less than a minute to get inside."

"Okay, but can I come in and look around?"

"No. Sorry, I can vouch for one person on each trip." He looked at Hardy. "Come on, man. We gotta get in there. Grab that suitcase."

As Hardy stepped out, Seth stuck his arm into the cab and handed Charlie four hundred dollars. "Here's the fare and the tip. Thanks for a great ride, Charlie. You got us here on time. That's all that matters. I wish you a wonderful life. Remember what I said…go past the station. Then all right turns until you reach a familiar highway." He shut the door and walked toward the station.

When Hardy lagged behind, Seth spun around. "Hardy, speed it up, man. Give me that suitcase. We have to be inside before midnight."

Hardy stopped. "Wait a minute. I'm not sure I wanna do this."

Seth grabbed the suitcase. "You can change your mind inside. You may be stuck out here for a long time if you leave now."

Hardy searched the parking lot. The cab grew smaller in the distance.

Seth whirled and walked fast. Quick footsteps sounded behind him.

Seth vouched for his guest with the guard at the station door, and then turned to Hardy.

"Come with me," He entered a room through a door marked *Private*, set the suitcase on the floor, and opened it. "We gotta change clothes. Better hurry if you want anything to eat before the train leaves."

26

"Why? What if I decide not to do this?" Hardy glanced inside the suitcase. "I don't want to wear that stuff. Why do I have to put on ugly clothes?"

Seth rolled his eyes. "You don't have to, but the guard will not allow you to leave this building dressed as a police officer. Whether you go or stay, you have to change clothes."

Five minutes later, the men walked out, their uniforms left inside the suitcase on the floor. Hardy looked at the grandfather clock in the corner of the station. "It's past midnight, but the train is still here."

Seth nodded. "The bar is across the station door. Nobody gets in after midnight. The train leaves at twelve-thirty sharp."

Hardy's face grew pink when he looked at his shirt, overalls, and boots. "I don't believe this. Tell me this is nothing but a bad dream."

"Okay, I'll tell you whatever you want." Seth spoke over his shoulder as he walked toward the food counter. "Then you can think about it every night in your prison cell for the next five years."

Hardy caught up, stopped in front of him, and pushed his angry face close. "What do you mean by *five* years?"

Seth stopped and showed an easy smile. "I was being kind. Earlier, you said you might get off with one year. But now, you're an escapee, a fugitive. If they go easy on you, you may get by with five years." He stepped around Hardy, went to the counter, and placed his order.

Hardy moved beside him. Seth motioned toward the lady behind the counter. "Hardy, this is Rhonda. She waits on customers, cooks the food, does all the cleaning…everything." Rhonda walked to the stove.

Hardy turned to Seth. What do you recommend?"

Seth answered without turning his head. "A sausage biscuit and coffee. It's the best they have."

"Why is that?"

"It's *all* they have."

Hardy frowned. "Okay, but… is it any good?"

"Depends on how hungry you are."

Hardy called out, "Hey, ma'am, I'll have the same."

Minutes later, Rhonda scooped the sausages from the cast-iron skillet on the wood-burning cook stove, slid them between the buttermilk biscuits, and brought the order wrapped in newspaper. "Unless you brought your own cups, you'll have to pay me for these. They're a nickel each, but they're made of good, solid glass."

When Seth looked at him, Hardy shrugged. "Sorry, Seth. I didn't have time to grab my wallet when we left the hospital."

Seth grinned, dug two old quarters from his pocket, and paid for the orders, including ten cents for the cups and another nickel for a tip. He stuffed the package in the bib pocket of his overalls and picked up the coffee. "I'm taking mine on the train."

Hardy nodded. "Me, too."

Seth looked at him, trying to act surprised. "So, you decided to get on the train? Once you do, there is no turning back."

"Sounds better than five years in the pen."

Seated on the train, the men ate their late dinner, or very early breakfast, in silence.

Finishing off his coffee, Hardy wiped his mouth on his sleeve and turned to Seth. "I have a lot of questions for you."

"I'm sure you do. I have a lot of answers, but *some* things I don't know. You'll learn a lot after you've lived at your new home for a while."

"Okay, let's start from the top. You told me before you're some kind of agent, and you had a mission."

"Yes. Each year, I have a mission to perform on my birthday. I find someone who needs to start over, and I offer that someone a whole new life."

Hardy turned up his hands. "How did you know where to find me?"

"A few days ago, I went to that hospital ER and told them my heart was bothering me. They took one look at my ID and asked the same question I always get, *Is this birthdate correct?* I'll skip the details, but they admitted me right away." Seth grinned. "I have no idea *why.*"

Hardy looked confused as he leaned toward Seth. "How did you know it was me who needed help?"

"I didn't know until I got to your room. Someone chained to a hospital bed needs help of some kind."

"What if I'd said *no*? Your mission fails?"

"My mission is to make the offer to someone who needs it and appears to deserve it. If the candidate says yes, I start the mission."

Hardy rubbed his chin. "And if he says *no*?"

"It's done. I offer. I don't pressure."

"Can't you tell me more about where I'm going?"

"I could. But I won't. I don't want you to form opinions or expectations about a place you've never seen."

"How could you know I haven't been there?"

"Want some more coffee? There's a pot in the caboose to help keep the engineer awake."

Hardy grabbed his mug and stood. "Lead the way."

The coffee pot sat steaming on the old cast iron stove in the empty caboose. They filled their mugs and settled at a table in the corner.

Hardy looked around. "I like it back here. I never knew what was in a caboose. But … I want to know how you faked your death to get out of the hospital."

Seth shrugged. "I can stop my breath and heartbeat for a few minutes without causing any damage. It's one of the tools I got when I became an agent for Mystique."

"Mystique?"

"That's where we're headed," Seth smiled big. "Your new home."

The young man drew a deep breath and let it go. "The more I hear, the stranger it gets. But there's one other thing I gotta know. How did you get the key for the handcuffs?"

Seth laughed. "Not much mystery in that one. I got lucky. One day, after the officer released you for physical therapy, he left the key on the wall shelf by your bed. As soon as you left for treatment, I called a locksmith and offered him a hundred bucks to make a copy right away. He was there and back in less than thirty minutes with the new key. I put the old one in the same spot on the shelf."

Hardy looked impressed. "That's not hard to believe after we made it from the hospital to here." He rubbed his chin. "I suppose anybody could get cop uniforms from a costume shop. But how did you get me out of my room without getting caught?"

Seth gripped his chin. "I had to do my homework on that one." He stood. "Let's return to our passenger car, and I'll tell you."

At their seats again, Seth grabbed a pillow from the overhead shelf. "I'll tell you about the hospital, but after this, I gotta rest for a while."

"The night-duty officers at the hospital made a shift change at eleven o'clock. Ten minutes before, the officer on duty would take his daily report to the downstairs coffee room and meet the relief man. They would look over the report—and shoot the bull—for about twenty minutes before the new man went to the duty post. I took advantage of that time to set up your escape."

"How about all those crazy, impossible things that happened in the cab on the way here?"

Seth stuffed the pillow behind him and smiled. "Classified."

Ninety minutes passed. Seth stood up. "We'll be stopping in a couple of minutes. I'm gonna wait by the door so I can be first in line."

"What? We're there already?"

Seth laughed. "No, no. We'll stop for about fifteen minutes to take on some water. But I have to *get rid* of some. There's a couple of outhouses." He walked to the door.

***

The train moved again. Hardy headed toward the caboose again. On the previous trip, he had little time to look around. Now, he walked the aisle between the rows of seats in the three passenger cars, taking a long step over each hitch that coupled the cars.

Hardy saw many empty seats. He counted seven people in the first car, and five in the next. No children, yet none appeared older than early twenties. Some talked just above a whisper, not loud enough for Hardy to understand. He waved.

No one responded. No one spoke to him. No one turned to look at him. He wondered if anyone knew he was there.

The third car sat empty. Except for Seth and Hardy, the train held twelve passengers.

A half-hour later, Hardy dropped into the seat beside Seth. "You know, this ride is not half bad. But I'm exhausted. How much longer is this trip?"

Seth opened one eye and mumbled, "Bout three hours."

Hardy returned to the empty passenger car and found a blanket and bunk beds. Within five minutes, he snored on the top bunk.

When a screeching noise roused Hardy, he did not open his eyes. He heard the noise again and then a sound like a freight train whistle. Someone shook him and called his name.

"Get up. We're here. Gotta leave the train."

Chapter Five

Hardy groaned but did not move. "Train? What train? I'm exhausted. I gotta get some sleep."

"Come on, man. We're home. Let's go."

After a long, deep breath, Hardy slid off the bed and looked through the open door. "Doesn't *look like* home."

"It does now. This is your new home. Come on, let's get out of here before this train takes off again."

Seth stepped off the train and turned to face Hardy. "Come on, man." Seth pointed at the wagon beside the tracks. "If you don't want to walk the next three miles, get in the buckboard. It has enough room. That one's bigger than most."

Hardy walked toward the big wooden wagon. While people climbed aboard, he recognized a few faces of the unfriendly, somber crowd from the passenger cars. Now, they laughed and joked with each other. They appeared eager about the ride, or perhaps about a life they'd never known.

Seth promised the *good life*. Still, Hardy could not appreciate the young crowd's excitement. But he would keep a neutral attitude until this new life proved itself. He climbed into the buckboard and sat on the last seat at the rear.

With the tailgate closed, the driver clucked at the two big mules and yelled, "Giddy Up." The big wagon rolled.

Hardy expected a teeth-rattling ride for as long as this trip would take and resigned himself to the jolt. But the ride surprised him. He studied the wooden seats, single boards attached only at each end. With no center supports, the seats' easy bounce created a cushioned ride.

While the mules trudged along, Hardy turned and watched the workers around the train. One crew filled the coal car while another pumped water into the boiler tank. He felt a new fondness for that old train.

Yeah, Seth had insisted this one-way trip meant a lifetime commitment. But Hardy figured any train that could bring him here could take him home someday.

A slim boy near the front of the wagon sat facing the other passengers. One look told Hardy the boy did not get here on the train. He had to be a local, wherever this place might be.

The boy pulled a harmonica from his overalls. "I'll play a little tune for everybody if you like."

Without waiting, he began *My Darling Clementine*. When he finished, his audience applauded.

"We want more," someone yelled.

Wearing a shy grin and pink face, he held up his instrument and shrugged. "Sorry, I'm just learning to play this. That's a new song and it's all I know. Want me to play it again?"

His fans laughed and clapped, prompting another performance.

No one spoke to Hardy during the buckboard ride, and a sudden thought struck him. *Seth is not in the wagon.* He glanced around to make sure and grew concerned. *Had Seth, the man who brought him here, deserted him when he needed him most?*

Young people bounced and laughed while the big wheels with steel tires rolled over bumps and through ruts and dips in the dirt road. The driver laughed with them and motioned at a shelf in a front corner, where a long-handled dipper in the water bucket made a musical splash as the wagon rolled.

The helper filled the dipper and handed it to the driver, who made gulping noises as he swallowed. The helper refilled the dipper often and passed it around. Several passengers remarked about the great taste of the water.

At the end of the ride, the driver parked the mules in a lot near the *Town Hall* sign next to the water trough. The mules satisfied their own thirst.

The driver's helper jumped off the buckboard and opened the tailgate. Hardy stepped aside to allow the ladies to exit first.

The helper placed the stepstool on the ground and offered his hand to all the ladies to help them down.

The men stepped down unassisted. With everyone out except Hardy and the driver, Hardy jumped off the end of the wagon.

The driver, an older man in overalls and a gray hat stood in the back of the wagon and raised his hand. "Ladies and gentlemen, welcome to Mystique, where most of us have lived since the day we came into this world. We're happy with our town and proud of it. We hope all of you will be happy here, also. Thank you for coming. God bless everyone."

Hardy looked around at the general store, butcher shop, meeting hall, church, barbershop, and school. Centered among them, a wagon yard offered hitching posts and horse troughs. Everything appeared neat, clean and well-maintained. Mystique reminded him of an outdoor movie set he'd seen in Tucson, Arizona, built to resemble a town more than a hundred years ago.

Here, the street ran between the church and school, disappearing into the distance behind the town. Rope swings hung from large tree limbs in the front yards of homes. Barns, clotheslines, henhouses, and outhouses graced the backyards.

He drew a deep breath as a memory returned. Years ago, his parents took him to visit his mother's cousin in a small town in rural Missouri. He celebrated his ninth birthday there, and the town offered little to do except lighting firecrackers or nights spent in the barnyard howling at the moon.

Hardy rubbed his chin. This little place offered a bit of entertainment but little else. He found interesting features like the spinning barbershop pole powered by the wind hitting a fan at the top. The residents had created an attraction that appeared to be a genuine old town. But Hardy doubted tourists would return for many visits.

"Hello there."

Hardy turned, surprised to see the buckboard driver. The man looked much bigger here than in the wagon, more than six feet tall, with muscles he had likely earned by hard work.

"Glad to meet you. I'm Maxwell. Everybody calls me Max."

Hardy shook his hand. "Hello, sir. I'm Hardy Brooke. Interesting little tourist attraction. How long has it been here?"

The man cocked his head and grinned but did not reply.

Hardy waved his hand toward the general store. "You live around here?"

Sweat ran down the older man's bushy, white sideburns. He removed his hat and wiped his face and head with a bandanna. He returned it to the bib pocket of his overalls, replaced the hat, and pointed down the street. "Yep. My place is a bit behind the town."

Hardy shrugged. "How far is the town?"

The man gestured toward the general store. "About that far."

Hardy turned a full circle. "This is it? How many people live here?"

Max stroked his chin. "We ain't counted them in a while, but I'd say upwards of four hundred people now. Some new ones moving in over the past few years. We might have to add on to the school and maybe build a bigger store or two. Ain't a small town anymore."

Hardy frowned. "Where does everybody work?"

"Well, son, most of 'em farm." He backed away and looked at Hardy. You're a good- size young man. You done any farmin'? Takes a lot of crops to feed this many people. And, of course, all the animals." He gazed at the sky above and beyond the buildings and nodded. "I got a few acres at my place. Some cows, one for milkin' and a few for beef. I got hogs, a couple of riding horses, and a good pair o' mules."

He pointed down the road while he talked, moving his hand back and forth. "I grow beans, corn, and potatoes. Gotta few peach trees, some apples, and a watermelon patch." He placed his hand on Hardy's shoulder. "If it sounds like I'm braggin'… well, I don't do that. I want you to know that if you set your mind to it and work hard, you can have all you need. So, when you're ready to start work, come and see me. I can sure find plenty for you to do. And if you need a place to stay, I got a bunkhouse on the side of the barn. You'll get to meet some other men workin' for me."

He dipped his head and touched the brim of his hat. "You think about all that and come to see me when you're ready to start. I'll treat you square. All the best to you, young man." He turned, strode to the buckboard, and drove off.

Hardy stood speechless. He did not want to be a farmer. Did this so-called town have no other jobs to offer? *I gotta get out of here, no matter what.*

People walked by in all directions, talked, and laughed, couples holding hands, munching apples, nuts, popcorn, and cookies. Hardy rubbed his belly. Hours had passed since he ate.

He walked to the little café across from the general store but stopped outside. He had no money and didn't know a soul in this so-called town. How could Seth desert him? No sign of him since they left the train. *If this is a test, I guess I failed.*

On the bench outside the café door, Hardy listened to happy customers inside. His stomach made mad, gurgling noises while the aroma of cooking meat drifted through an open window.

Ten minutes proved to be all Hardy could handle. He opened the door and stepped in. Maybe the owner would consider giving him a job in the kitchen, waiting tables, or sweeping the floor. Anything.

"Hey, Hardy. Over here."

Hardy looked around. He scanned the tables. Someone waved and showed a giant smile. Two steps closer told Hardy what he wanted to know.

Seth motioned for him to sit and introduced him to two other men at the table. Though friendly and pleasant, they had little to say.

Seth slapped Hardy on the back. "Welcome to Mystique. Would you let me buy dinner for you?"

Hardy shrugged. He spoke above the sound of his grumbling stomach. "Okay, since we're good friends, I'll accept."

While the men tackled their plates, intermittent sounds of music came through the front window. "When we're done, let's go out and see who's playing?" Hardy said.

The four men joined the gathering crowd in the open square across from the café, where musicians brought instruments, chairs, and small kegs to sit on while they performed. People sat on the grass and waited.

After they tuned guitars, fiddles, and a banjo, the small band surprised Hardy with their talent. The crowd clapped and whistled after each tune.

Hardy's parents had been big country-western fans, and he heard that music often as he grew. But this band played songs that seemed very old, including a few sacred tunes like *Rock of Ages*. Maybe they wanted to respect the image this old town conveyed.

When the band took a break, Hardy turned to Seth. "I guess I have to find a place to sleep tonight. Where should I go? And how do I pay for it?"

With his eyes half closed, Seth rubbed his chin. "I know someone who would likely put you up for the night without charge and possibly … feed you breakfast tomorrow. Have you met the mayor of Mystique? Mayor Miller?"

Hardy brightened. "No, but I'd like to. How do I find him?"

"Well, it's about a mile-and-a-half from here." Seth leaned toward him. "Can you ride a horse?"

"I can."

Seth angled his head toward him. "I mean … are you a *good* rider. If not, we may have a bit of a problem."

Hardy spread his hands. "I had my own horse a few years ago. I'm a pretty darn-good rider. Just tell me how to get there and find me a horse."

"I have one you can borrow for a day or two."

A half-hour later, Seth pointed at an intersection. "You see the dirt road that runs alongside the schoolhouse and leads out of town? That's Never-Ending Road. It will get you there."

That dirt road? Hardy had seen nothing but dirt roads since he left the train. In fact, when he looked out the windows of the train, he saw nothing but dirt roads all the way here. But dirt roads were best for riding, and what a great feeling to be on a well-trained horse once more. He had missed riding and told himself he had not lied to Seth. When he turned fourteen, Hardy's parents gave him a horse as a birthday gift. He swallowed hard as he remembered.

Six months after his birthday, his parents accepted a great offer for their home in the country and moved into a subdivision. Hardy's horse-owning days came to an abrupt end.

Today, he sat tall in the saddle, looked around, and found beautiful country for riding. He wanted to make the ride much longer, take the horse past his destination, turn around and do it once more. But the sun hovered above the horizon, and he could see the big sign for Miller's Place ahead on the left.

He slowed the horse to an easy walk and followed the wagon track toward the barn.

When he rode past the farmhouse, a lazy hound struggled up from his nap on the rear porch and announced Hardy's arrival. Chickens squawked and scattered. The rear screen door squeaked open and slapped shut.

Hardy stopped the horse near the barn. Footsteps echoed from the porch as he slid off the saddle. Someone stopped behind him.

"Didn't expect to see you so soon Hardy. Glad you took me up on the job offer."

Chapter Six

Hardy moaned as he heard the yell. "Rise and shine. We got a great day ahead and a lot of work to do."

Half awake, he grabbed the rail of the bunkbed and eased up, straining to keep his eyes open. "What time is it?"

Someone said, "It's *daytime*. That's what it is."

A giant rooster strutted past the open bunkhouse door and crowed louder than any rooster Hardy ever heard or imagined. He rubbed his face and splashed water on it from the pan on the crude shelf next to his bunk. No need to get dressed. He'd slept in his clothes. He pulled on his boots and headed for the outhouse.

Three minutes later, Hardy tapped on the back door of the farmhouse. At the briefing last night after dinner, that's what Nelda, the lady of the house, told him to do each morning if he wanted breakfast.

"Say your name, and wait for my reply," she told him. "Wipe your feet, come on in, wash your hands, take off your hat, and sit down at the table."

Fully awake, Hardy's stomach sounded as if it wanted to start a fight while he waited for Nelda's reply. When he opened the door, Nelda yelled, "You didn't say your name. Go out and start over."

He closed the door, knocked once more, and yelled, "Hardy!"

"Well, what're you waiting for? Come in and get fed."

He wiped his feet, washed his hands in the pan by the stove, removed his hat, and pulled out a chair at the table.

Nelda dipped her head toward him. "Good morning, Hardy. We waited for you …" She looked at the other three men at the table. "Mister Miller, Barney, Cecil, and me." She stared at Hardy. "We waited because this is your first day on the job. We will not do that in the future. Next time you're late, we will consider it rude, and we have no breakfast for rude people. And … we always thank the Lord for our meals." She nodded at her husband. "Maxwell."

She bowed her head.

After Maxwell's short prayer, Nelda spread her hands and looked at the food on the table. "As you can see, we have eggs, bacon, and some good homemade pork sausage. There's gravy and buttermilk biscuits and always lots of coffee. We've got plenty for everybody, and you'll find cream and fresh-churned butter on the table too."

She glanced at the big grandfather clock in the living room. "It's five o'clock. You got a half-hour. Better get to it." She sat and grabbed a biscuit.

***

When the sun parked straight overhead, Hardy stopped the mule team that had dragged him behind a plow all morning long. For many hours, he tripped, stumbled, and staggered through the fresh-plowed earth and mule manure, yelling *gee, haw,* or *whoa,* mule talk for *right, left,* and *stop.*

That's what Max taught him after breakfast this morning. He also said, "You have to be the boss of the team, not the other way around." But Max forgot to tell the mules who was boss.

Hardy gazed at the few furrows he'd plowed in the field. One appeared almost straight, but he could not believe Mister Miller would be happy with that. As the new man behind the team, he soon discovered the mules knew much more about

42

plowing than he ever wanted to *learn*. This was not merely the worst job in his lifetime. It was the worst one he could possibly *imagine* in *any* lifetime.

He glanced over at the hayfield. His mouth fell open. Barney and Cecil had stopped bailing hay. They sat on bales in the shade of a tree, dug cloth bags from somewhere in their overalls, and started gobbling down biscuits.

Hardy shaded his eyes for a better look. When Cecil bit off a hunk, the biscuit appeared loaded with sausage and egg. But Hardy's life got worse when the two guys drank from small glass bottles they also pulled from their overalls. It looked like apple cider. Hardy loved apple cider.

Nothing about it was fair. Barney and Cecil sat on bales in the shade, stuffing their guts, laughing, and talking between bites. Nobody told Hardy it was lunchtime. And where did those two get all that food?

Dropping the reins, he told the mules to stay, and walked to the hayfield. He stopped next to the other two men.

"Afternoon, Hardy," Barney said. "I don't see how you could go without lunch. I gotta have something in my gut by this time of day, or I won't hold up to work."

His words made Hardy's stomach growl again. "Well, I'm starving. Where and how do I find lunch? Do I have to go to the house and ask for it?"

Cecil chuckled. "That won't work. You gotta pound on the door and yell at Nelda, *Bring me some lunch. Right now.*"

Barney and Cecil laughed. Hardy's face grew purple while he glared at Cecil.

Barney slapped his knee. "After breakfast, you gotta grab it, stuff it in a sack and bring it with you." He jerked his thumb toward Cecil. "Nelda reminded us this morning, but I guess it was before you got there. Sorry, man. When everybody's out of the kitchen, what's left goes to the chickens and the dog. And to the hogs if anything's left after that."

Hardy removed his hat and wiped his sweating face on his sleeve, and then replaced his hat. "I wish somebody had told me. The last thing I want to do is go without a meal."

Barney swallowed, looked up, and grinned. "I'm surprised you'd say that."

"Well, Barney, don't you think I get hungry, also?" Hardy grumbled.

Barney leaned sideways to look past Hardy and drawled, "Well, I reckon so, but I figured the last thing you'd want is your pair o' mules wandering away."

Hardy whirled around. The mules dragged the plow toward the creek. "Oh, no. I forgot to water them," he yelled as he ran off.

***

After Hardy had his fill at supper, Nelda told him to wait in the bunkhouse because … "Mister Miller wants to talk with you when he gets in from town."

He waited but needed a good night's sleep more than anything else. It wasn't fair to expect an exhausted man with a full gut to stay awake for long.

Nothing had gone right today. Nothing. At noon, when Max looked up from the potato patch and saw the mules at the creek, he cut across the hayfield to get there and disconnected the plow. When the mules had their fill of water, he reconnected the plow and drove the team back to the field. Max did not appear upset but said little to Hardy at the time.

Hardy stood up from the bunk as Max walked into the bunkhouse. "Hello, Mister Miller."

The man smiled. "Just call me Max." He cleared his throat. "I'll get right to the point. I'm a pretty fair man, and I usually start my help at twenty-five dollars a month." He pulled four quarters from his pocket and held them out. "But here's a bit more than a day's pay. Quite honestly, Hardy, the work here does not seem to fit you. I wish you the best."

Hardy's mouth fell open. "Twenty-five dollars a month? Are you serious?"

"Yes. Farming is pretty hard work. So, I pay a bit more than most other places around here." He shook hands with Hardy and slapped him on the shoulder. "You can spend the night here if you want. But you will need to be out early in the morning. I got a new guy supposed to be here at five-thirty." He turned to go but stopped at the door. "In case you forgot, tomorrow is Sunday. Can I expect to see you in church?"

Hardy's mouth dropped open. He stared with a puzzled face but did not answer.

During the night, his thoughts woke him many times. *Sure wish Max had said to leave after breakfast.* Even so, when the sun offered the first promise of daylight, and the giant rooster crowed to take credit for it, Hardy jumped off the bunk bed. He splashed water on his face while a horse whinnied in front of the barn. The new man was here.

Hardy led his horse out of the barn and saddled him in the morning light. He said hurried goodbyes to everyone he saw and mounted the horse. When he reached the road in front of Miller's Place, Hardy's heart told him to turn left, to ride the horse down Never-Ending Road, as Seth called it, to see what was out there. To ride a good horse on an unfamiliar trail, is an experience a rider could get no other way.

Hardy's stomach disagreed and wanted breakfast.

Chapter Seven

With mixed feelings, Hardy turned right. On the horse Seth lent him for a day or two, Hardy now rode back to town a day-and-a-half later, down the Never-Ending Road that brought him here.

He wanted to tell Max how much he hated plowing but thought better of it. Getting along with the mayor of Mystique might be an advantage in the future.

Many things played through Hardy's mind while he rode. Mystique existed as more than an old town. It existed as a world of its own. This *old world* may be great for the people who live here. But Hardy told himself he could never adapt. In spite of the consequences, he had to return to his other world, the *real* world.

Hardy tied the horse near the water trough in front of the town café. He started for the door, jingling the four quarters in his pocket, and hoping he had enough to make his stomach happy.

When he opened the café door, Seth yelled, "Hey, Hardy, over here." He waved from the same table as before, but today, he sat alone. He stood. They shook hands and sat.

Hardy rubbed his belly. "I didn't have breakfast. Glad to find this place open on Sunday."

"Yeah, from six till nine on Sunday mornings." He angled his head toward the window. "I saw you ride up. Didn't expect to see you this early. Is Handsome Devil okay?"

Hardy's brow wrinkled. "Handsome Devil? You mean … Mister Miller?"

"No, no. My horse." Seth laughed.

Hardy laughed with him. "I didn't know his name. But I like it. He's a great horse. Wish he was mine."

Seth grinned. "He's not. But it's good to see you. I hoped you would be here today. I'm sure Max and Nelda will be here for church. So, you'll be riding home with them after Sunday service?"

He took a deep breath. "No, I won't be doing that."

Seth's eyes widened. "How will you get to work tomorrow? Sorry, Hardy. I'm gonna need my horse by tomorrow morning." He spread his hands and stared.

"I didn't have breakfast this morning, Seth. Let me turn in my order." He glanced at the menu sign on the wall. Delighted he could get a full breakfast for ten cents, Hardy motioned for the waitress, placed his order, and turned to his friend.

"Seth, I gotta ask you about Never-Ending Road. Why do you call it that?"

Seth shrugged. "There's no sign on the road, but that's what everybody calls it."

"Okay, how long is it?"

"No idea. Never been down that far."

"Well, I'm sure somebody's been down there. It *has* to have an end."

Seth leaned toward him. "What about *you*? Did your *job* have an end?"

Hardy felt his face flush. "Let's just say I don't have to be there tomorrow."

"Oh? You got the day off? Or the job didn't work out?"

"It didn't work for Max, and it didn't work for me. But we parted friends."

Seth nodded. "Making friends with him counts for a lot. Anything else in mind? Another job, maybe?"

Hardy half smiled. "I don't have many options at this point. Anything you want to suggest?"

"I know a good place to start. Would you like to go to church with me? Service is at ten-thirty, and the pastor usually says the last *Amen* by noon."

Hardy looked at his overalls and snickered. "You can't be serious. I'd be embarrassed to walk into a hog pen dressed like this."

The young lady delivered Hardy's breakfast. He thanked her and gave her a nickel for a tip. She blushed. "Thank you so much." She hurried away.

While Hardy ate breakfast, Seth talked. "Going to church is strictly up to you. I won't press it. But if you go, you'll see lots of other men there in overalls."

"Thanks for your help, Seth. It'll take a while to adjust if I *can*. But first, I have to find a place to sleep tonight. Any ideas?"

"Church is the place to start. I don't mean to pressure you, but most business owners in this village will be there today. Your best bet is to get acquainted with them, and I can introduce you."

Hardy swallowed the last bite of breakfast, swallowed the last of his coffee, wiped his hands, and stood. "You've been a good friend. I appreciate all you did for me and still do. But this place won't work for me. I want to go home, and I'll face the consequences, no matter what they are." He glanced around at other customers in the café.

Seth looked at the ceiling then straight at Hardy. "I told you several times … this is a lifetime commitment and—"

"Let's take this outside if you don't mind." Hardy cut in.

Outside, Seth patted Handsome Devil on the neck while the horse showed his affection.

Hardy gripped Seth's shoulder. "You're a good friend, and I know you told me over and over about the lifetime commitment. But I don't care. Just tell me how to get home, and I'll be gone as soon as I can."

"It's not going to happen, Hardy. I'm not keeping you here. No one can send you back, and *I* would not do it even if I could."

"I'll find a way. *Nothing* is impossible. The people here are great. They help me, and I like them. But I cannot stand the thought of living this way for the rest of my life. It's like a return trip to the dark ages. They're still using animals here to do the work of tractors, trucks, cars, and machines. These poor people chop wood for fuel to cook their meals and heat their homes. They use hand tools to dig wells and bring the water up in buckets or pitcher pumps. They don't have electricity or indoor plumbing." Hardy frowned. "Using an outhouse is disgusting. I can't …"

Seth caught Hardy's arm. "Hold on, young man. Most of what you said is true, but your attitude is way off track. The people you meet here are genuine. They are comfortable and true friends because they care about each other."

Hardy turned away. Seth stepped in front of him and looked into his eyes. "You won't find a police force here or a sheriff. We have almost no crime. When we do, it's most often someone from your world stealing from one of us, and I haven't seen that in many years. They don't get away with it."

He grabbed Hardy's shoulders and pulled him close. "These are the happiest people I've met. Don't try to change them."

Hardy hung his head, shook it, and looked up. "I didn't mean to insult you or anybody else. The people I've met have been more than fair with me, but I don't know if I can adjust to this lifestyle."

Seth released him. "You've been here barely more than a day. Before you try something crazy that won't work anyway, do your best here for a month. Maybe you'll change your mind about us."

"It's not the people, Seth. It's the lifestyle. How many years have these people been living like this? You know what life is like in my world. Don't you want to give your friends here the same advantages you've seen there?"

"No, Hardy. I do not. Your so-called *advantages* come with lots of *disadvantages* that would change everything these people are, all they have, all they believe in." held up his index finger. "Think about this. If you and your neighbor across the street got along, you would not have been shot in the butt, chained to a bed in a hospital, or faced time in prison. And … you would not be here now."

After a moment of silence, Hardy said, "Okay, I get your point. But I have to get a job."

"Ask the blacksmith. I see him in church every Sunday."

"Can I talk to him today?" Hardy cocked his head and looked into Seth's eyes. "Do you know something I don't?"

Seth smiled. "A *lot* of things."

"Okay, I'll go to church. But if I feel out of place because of how I'm dressed, I'll get up and walk out. You want us to sit apart? I don't want to embarrass you."

"You can sit by me. It won't be the *first* time I've been embarrassed."

Hardy's face grew warm as they both laughed.

Chapter Eight

Church bells rang as Hardy and Seth walked next door for the service. Seth seemed calm. Hardy felt uncomfortable and out of place, staring at his dirty overalls and beat-up shoes. Up ahead, he watched Max and Nelda walk into the church. Max wore a blue suit and tie. Nelda came in a dress of bright colors, white shoes, and a small hat with a flower. Hardy liked her despite some of her ways. She was one tough woman, yet kind and helpful to people who respected her. Hardy did.

Seth leaned toward him and whispered, "The men in overalls will be here." He jerked his head toward the wagons. "Take a look at the wagon yard, known in your world as a parking lot."

Hardy saw two men step out of a wagon and start toward the church. Both wore overalls, but they were *clean* overalls. Each man also wore a clean, white shirt.

Hardy whispered back, "I don't like this. But I'll go in if we sit in the last row."

Hardy and Seth attended the service from the back pew. When the congregation sang along with the church band, Seth joined in. Hardy sat speechless with his arms folded. He recognized most of the people in the band from the concert he saw on his first day here.

When the crowd passed around the preacher's hat, Seth dropped in a quarter. Hardy considered the three quarters and a dime in his pocket, with no idea when or how he would get more. He felt a drop of sweat form on his forehead while he stared at the ceiling and placed nothing into the hat. After the service, Seth and Hardy waited outside while the crowd ambled out as if Sunday afternoon would last a week.

Seth knew most of them and introduced many to Hardy while he watched the members gather in small groups outside. Someone would say to the group, "Come on over to our place for dinner." Hardy wanted to accept every invitation but declined. He had necessary business to take care of this afternoon.

A short, muscular man came out of the church and weaved his way through the crowd without talking to anyone. Seth waved to get his attention and motioned for Hardy to follow. They caught up to him, formed their own small circle a few steps from the crowd, and made introductions. Seth wasted no time.

"I hear you're overloaded with work, Sam. Hardy is looking for a job. It could work out for both of you."

Sam stared at Hardy. "You ever worked for a blacksmith or farrier?"

Hardy scrunched his face. "No. But I can learn either one."

"A farrier shoes horses and mules. You know anything about horses? If you're afraid of 'em, I can't use you," Sam said.

Hardy lowered his head. "I know what a farrier is. I had my own horse a few years ago, and I love to ride."

Sam grinned and shrugged. "I need help." His eyes scanned Hardy's overalls. "It's a dirty job, but you can wear what you have on."

Seth covered his mouth and snickered as the blacksmith yelled over his shoulder, "See you in the morning."

Hardy started after him. "Hey, Sam, I need a place to stay. Do you know of anything?"

Sam turned to face him. "I've got a bunkroom at the back of the shop where I slept for a couple of years when I first started my business. It ain't much, but it's big enough to sleep in."

He dug a key from his pocket and tossed it to Hardy. "That will get you in. Be at my shop ready for a hard day's work at 6 o'clock tomorrow morning."

***

At 5 o'clock on Monday morning, Hardy ordered breakfast at the café, then rubbed his eyes and thought about everything that happened yesterday afternoon.

After the blacksmith left, the pastor and his wife stopped in front of Seth and Hardy. "Your name is Hardy, I'm told. I'm Pastor Quake, and this is Missus Quake. My first name is Conrad, but after a fiery sermon, folks like to call me *Earth Quake*."

Five minutes later, the Missus invited Hardy and Seth to dinner. Hardy stood straight with his hands on his hips and shook his head until the lady caught his arm. She stared up at him.

"Mister Hardy, if you and Brother Seth have other plans for dinner, we understand. If something else is bothering you, we don't want to insist. But we'll be disappointed. You seem like such a nice young man."

Seth nodded. "You're right, Sister. He is a nice young man, but he feels out of place in his overalls."

Her mouth dropped open. "That's no reason to turn down our invitation. If you can wear those to church, you can wear them to our house for dinner."

Hardy couldn't decide if her remark made him feel better or worse, but he recognized his limited choices. Seth would likely go *with* him or *without* him. The café had closed for the day, and Hardy did not want to do without dinner.

Within minutes, Hardy enjoyed a comfortable ride in the back seat of the carriage while the pastor drove home. Seth followed on Handsome Devil.

***

Hardy found yesterday's dinner a real treat. He'd always liked fried chicken, homemade biscuits, and apple pie. While he stuffed his gut, Hardy assumed the after-dinner conversation would focus on church activities or church members he did not know. Instead, the pastor talked for more than an hour about squirrel hunting, mountain lions, and his prize coonhounds.

When the pastor drove his guest back to town, he asked Hardy many questions about his background and beliefs in the Almighty. Hardy found most questions a bit awkward. He'd been to church a few times but had not thought about it as a commitment or regular part of his life. Relieved when he stepped out of the carriage, he inserted his key into the lock at the blacksmith shop.

Examining the bunkroom where Sam had lived for two years, Hardy smiled … glad to find a door he could shut for privacy. He could hang his clothes on several large nails sticking out from the walls. The shelves on the wall near the bed would be handy for odds and ends. Not exactly a closet, he told himself, but this will work for a while.

In the front corner of the room, a small table offered a place to have a meal or write letters. A sudden thought hit him. He had nobody to write to and, perhaps, never would again. For the first time, he realized he'd seen no post office or mailboxes.

Hardy tried the bed, a simple but sturdy, shallow wooden box about two feet above the floor. He did not expect the bed to have sheets or a blanket but was glad to see a mattress.

He lifted one end of the mattress, squeezed it, and rubbed his fingers across the ticking to feel the stuffing inside. He lifted

54

the mattress and smelled it. Now, he knew a featherbed, like the one he'd slept on in his great-grandmother's house when he was a boy.

He turned, lifted the latch, and opened the back door of the bunkroom. "Aha," he said. "This could be very handy." A trail led directly to the outhouse.

***

Hardy managed supper last night, but his belly arrived empty at the café in the morning. Splurging again for a full breakfast, and another fifteen cents including the tip, he wolfed it down. He would show up early on the first day of a new job. Impress the boss.

He glanced at the café clock on his way out. "Five-thirty-five," he said. After the 10-minute walk, he reached for his key to Sam's Blacksmith Shop but dropped the key back into his pocket. Through the walls came the unmistakable sound of a heavy hammer pounding iron.

Sunlight streamed into the shop when he opened the door. With a huge grin, the new boss yelled, "Good morning, Hardy." He angled his head at a hook on the wall. "Grab an apron and come on over here."

The full-length apron reminded Hardy of the aprons he wore as a teenager when he worked at a supermarket. But those aprons were cotton. This one was leather and much heavier.

For the next hour, Hardy stood near the fire pit and worked the bellows. With the forced air, the coals grew hot enough to soften the iron bars Sam pounded into shape.

During a short break, Hardy and Sam sat on a bench and talked. Sam drank a cup of coffee from the pot on the fire pit grill. Hardy gulped down a dipper of water from the bucket on a shelf in the corner and jerked his thumb toward the fire behind them.

"The shoes you're making must be for ponies. I've never seen any that small."

Sam grinned. "They're mule shoes. Next time you see a mule, look at his feet. They're a lot smaller than horse feet."

Hardy did not reply. After that one day of plowing, he never wanted another close look at a mule's feet. He started to change the subject, but Sam left the bench.

"Okay, break's over."

Hardy reached for his apron and groaned. Fatigued muscles in his arms made it tough for him to tie the apron behind his back.

Chapter Nine

Dog-tired and half asleep, Hardy plopped down on the chair in the café and rested his elbows on the table. Seth stopped by the blacksmith shop this afternoon, the first time Hardy had seen him in over two weeks. He asked to meet for supper at the café. Now, Hardy hoped he could stay awake long enough to have a conversation with his friend.

A week before, Jeff, the chef and owner of the café, tied a string of bells on the front door. When he worked alone, he knew when someone came in or left. The bells jingled, and Hardy looked up. No one came in but someone left. A minute later, another jingle when Seth walked in wearing a huge smile as if he had good news to share.

When he reached the table, Hardy stood, and they shook hands. But this time, Seth gave him a big hug. "Good to see you, buddy. How's life treating you?"

Hardy sat again. "I've had better days, but most of all, I'm worn down from the job."

Seth sat across from him. "If you think about it, I'll bet you'll realize you had tougher jobs than this one."

Hardy frowned. "You'd lose your bet. I thought plowing with mules was a tough job. This one is less aggravating, but the work is even harder. Sometimes at the end of the day, I hit the sack and forget about having a meal."

The waitress stopped at the table. The men ordered, then stared at each other after she walked away. After a long, dead silence, Hardy folded his hands on the table and leaned forward.

"Seth, every time we get together for a meal, it seems I complain about my job. I don't want to do that now, but if I ever dreamed of becoming a blacksmith, that dream is now a nightmare."

Seth rubbed his chin. "Someday, *maybe someday soon,* this town is going to need another blacksmith. Could be a real future for you."

Hardy sat up straight. "If that's what you call a future, I don't want one." After a few seconds of silence, Hardy said, "I don't mind hard work, but day after day, I get more tired of the grind, heat, and dirt."

"How long you been on that job? Seems like barely a couple of weeks."

"It'll be three weeks tomorrow, and if I had something else lined up, I'd quit. Don't get me wrong. Sam's a great guy and is good to work for and *with.* But the job wears me down. I can't see that as a long-term job, much less a career."

The waitress brought their dinners and flashed a big smile at Hardy. "It's always good to see you, Hardy. Anything else I can do for you?"

"That's all for today. Thank you, Caroline."

She walked away. Hardy dug into his plate.

When the men finished their meals, Seth wiped his hands, dropped the napkin on the table, and stared at Hardy. "Okay, my friend, you don't like your new job, and I'm not sure what I can say to change your mind."

"I don't want to change my mind, Seth. You helped me get the job I have, and I'm grateful. Could you help me get another one?"

"I'll help if I can, Hardy, *if* we can do it my way. I asked Sam to consider you for the job, and I want you to be fair with

58

him. You have to give Sam a week's notice, or more, before you quit."

Hardy nodded. "I'll do that."

"Thank you. What kind of work do you like?"

"For a couple of years, I worked in men's clothing and then in the hardware section of a large store that sold just about everything. I'll try the general store if you'll introduce me to the owners and recommend me. That is if you know them."

Seth smiled. "The people who own that business are friends of mine. If you'll attend church Sunday morning, I can introduce you to them, and we'll see what happens."

Hardy thanked him and threw up his hands. "Of course, if I change jobs, I'll need a new place to stay. So, I'll have to work on that, and I have not seen a *For Rent* sign anywhere around here. Can you tell me how to find a place to live?"

Seth stood. "Just mention that to the Walkers when you discuss the job. Maybe they can come up with something."

***

After Seth introduced Hardy to Wayne and Wanda Walker, Mrs. Walker invited Hardy and Seth for Sunday dinner at their home. After dinner, they would go to the store and discuss the job.

For Hardy, nothing had gone this well for him in a long while. He would go along to get along. But no one would change his mind. He would leave this town at the first possible opportunity.

At the store, Wayne's first remark brought another surprise. "I could use a man tall enough to reach the top shelves for cleaning and stocking."

Hardy moved next to the high shelves, placed his hand on the top shelf, and grinned.

Wayne returned the grin. "You just might work out. You must be a bit over six feet tall."

Hardy smiled. "Yes, sir, six feet, two inches."

Wayne nodded at Seth then looked at Hardy. "We heard you need a place to stay." He glanced at the ceiling. "We have a small apartment upstairs. Take a look and see if it'll work for you."

After a ten-minute tour of the loft apartment, Hardy grew excited. Back downstairs, Wanda Walker pulled a small note from her pocket. "This is what we will pay you starting out."

Hardy looked at the paper, at her, and once more at the paper. He laughed. "But… that says *one dollar a day*. Must be something wrong."

Wanda shrugged. "We typically start new help at eighty cents a day, but we're hoping you'll work out better than some others have."

"How many hours a day?"

Wayne cut in. "We try to limit it to ten hours a day, six days a week. But when we get swamped, we'll have to go a bit more than ten hours. And … you'll get paid for that extra time."

Wanda pointed up. "You won't have to pay for your room upstairs. But you will have to furnish your own firewood for the cook stove and to heat the room in cold weather."

Conversation died. Hardy glanced at Seth, hoping for help. Seth rolled his eyes at the ceiling.

Hardy opened his hand for the paper. Mrs. Walker dropped it into his hand and looked into his eyes. "Tell us your problem, please."

Hardy glanced once more at the paper. "It's hard to adjust. Jobs in my previous life paid many times more than here."

Wayne cleared his throat. "We've hired people from that place. Despite the differences, people keep coming to *our* place, not the other way around. Prices for everything here are many times lower. You can buy a decent home here for less than a thousand dollars, and it likely has three acres or more to go with it."

"But this job pays less than the one I have."

Wayne sighed. "If you refuse to adjust, life here is going to be a real struggle. But we gave you a choice. In a couple of years, you may turn out to be a fine blacksmith. All the best."

He snapped his fingers, opened his palm, and held it under Hardy's fist. "The paper, please."

Chapter Ten

Hardy jerked his fist away. "Sorry, I'll take the job…if it's still open." Wayne and Wanda stared at each other.

"I'm not sure the job's still open," Wanda said. She turned to Hardy. "If you make so much more at your other job, you may work a week for us, then quit and go back to blacksmithing."

Hardy swallowed. "Sam is a great guy, and he's paying me twelve cents an hour because he knows the work is hot, hard, and heavy. I'll do a great job for you here. That's a promise."

Wayne took Wanda's hand. "Maxwell Miller is a pretty good judge of character. A couple of weeks ago after church, he recommended Hardy in case we needed somebody at the store. Maybe we should give him a chance if he wants the job."

Hardy nodded. "I really do, sir. I'll do everything to be the best employee you ever had. But I'm a fair man, and I want to give Sam a week's notice."

Wanda smiled. "You're hired. We expect to see you here one week from tomorrow at seven."

Wayne shook hands with Hardy. "If you like the room, you can move in next Saturday. No need to wait till after your first day on the job."

"Thanks." Hardy said. "The only thing I have to move is me."

***

On the following Saturday, Hardy walked into the general store with a large smile. Wayne looked up from his work.

"Hello, Hardy. Good to see you. It's just two o'clock. I thought you had to work till three on Saturdays."

"Since it was my last day on the job, I left an hour early."

Wayne angled his head. "I hope all went well between you and Sam. He's a good man and works as hard as anybody I've met."

Hardy breathed deep. "All is fine between Sam and me. Monday morning, when I told him I'd be leaving, he was pretty upset. He said he'd spent three weeks training me and paying me a good salary to learn. To say the least, he was not happy I quit. We didn't talk much during the week, and he worked me harder than ever. But this morning, he apologized and wished me the best."

Wayne brought a key from his pocket and held it out. "This is for your room." He brought out another key. "This one is for the store and the gate that leads to the backyard. See you Monday morning no later than seven. I suggest you buy a pocket watch as soon as you have enough money. I'll give you a good price."

Wanda motioned her head at Hardy's overalls. "When you can afford it, we can also give you a good price on new clothes."

Hardy blushed. "Thank you. I'll certainly keep that in mind."

"We want to help you settle into your new life. Have you been to the barbershop?" Wanda asked.

"Uh, no. Do I need a haircut?"

"Maybe not, but the barbershop has a bathtub with curtains all around for privacy. I don't know how much the barber charges for that. We use our own bathtub at home. But if you want a bath Monday morning before you start to work, we'll pay for it."

Hardy blushed, nodded, and went upstairs.

He studied his new home. What would he need? He sat in the big chair with the handmade cushion and found it comfortable. He found the small chair at the tiny, two-person dining table less than comfortable. But he would spend little time on that one.

A big metal bucket with three sticks of firewood waited next to the cast-iron stove. He made a mental note to bring up more firewood.

Hardy stared at the big metal tub sitting on a sturdy waist-high cabinet at the other end of the room. On his first visit a week ago, Wanda called it a *washtub*. The tub seemed too large for washing dishes and much too small for a bathtub, but he chose not to expose his ignorance by asking questions. When he considered the rope that stretched across the room near the end wall, Hardy laughed aloud, smacked his head with his hand, and uttered, "Duh, a clothesline."

On Saturday evening, Hardy sat at the café and enjoyed dinner with a blacksmith customer he met a few days ago. When he revealed he no longer worked there, the man looked surprise. "You quit? I've always wanted to be a blacksmith but had nobody to teach me. You think Sam might hire me?"

"Well, Virgil, if you'll meet me at church tomorrow morning, I'll introduce you to Sam. Tell him what you told me. It's hot and dirty work, but he's a good teacher and a great guy to work with."

***

At 5 o'clock on Monday morning, Hardy waited in line at the café and talked to friends and strangers about his new job. Many congratulated him and welcomed him to the community.

"I just want to fit in," he said. "I'll do everything I can to make this new life work out." He felt uneasy saying those words. But the whole truth would make his life much worse.

At breakfast, he shared a table with two men he'd met outside. The man who talked most outside now spoke the most *inside*.

"Well, young man, I think you figured out the best way to make friends is to *be* one. When you agree with someone, let 'em know. When you don't, show respect."

Hardy wanted to sit, talk, and listen for another hour. He also wanted to be first in line at the barbershop and hoped the barber would fill the tub with fresh, warm water this morning. But before his bath, Hardy would go to the store and try to buy new clothes on credit.

At five-thirty, Hardy unlocked the store and walked in, surprised to see the Walkers arranging items and stocking shelves with new merchandise. The two top shelves appeared nearly bare. Hardy assumed they left those shelves for him.

"Good morning, Wayne, and Wanda. The door was locked, so I thought I was the first one here.".

Wanda grinned. "We keep the door locked until six. Some people like to come in after breakfast, some *before* breakfast, and hang around until the store opens. They talk about anything and everything, which means we don't get our work done."

Hardy nodded. "Understood. I don't want to interrupt anything, but I need some new clothes. Can we arrange something until I get paid?"

Wayne beckoned Hardy to the back of the store. "Let me show you something." Wayne brushed his hand across a shelf of pants. "What do you think of these?"

Hardy's mouth dropped open. He could not believe what he saw. He picked up a pair of pants. "These are … blue jeans. I did not expect to find these here."

"No, I didn't think you would. Some people from your world show up wearing these. Wanda and I bought a couple pairs from those people and took them to a tailor here in town. We knew it was a gamble, but we have them in several sizes, hoping they'll catch on."

Hardy nodded. "Mister Walker, I've worn jeans for as long as I can remember, and so did most other people. I bet you will sell more of these than any other pants in the store."

Wayne laughed and looked at Wanda. "You hear that, Honey?"

Minutes later, Hardy walked into the barbershop with new jeans, shirt, socks, underwear, and a hat. A slick-bald man worked a pitcher pump installed next to the big metal bathtub. With the tub half full, he brought water from the cast-iron cook stove in the back of the shop and dumped six bucketsful of steaming water into the tub.

He removed his glove, stuck his hand into the water, and nodded. He smiled, turned to Hardy, and offered a handshake. "Don't believe we met. I'm Barry, the barber." He looked at Hardy's new clothes. "You here for a bath?"

"I'm Hardy, and yes, I am."

"It's a bit expensive because it takes a lot of water and a lot of work for me. I have to charge fifteen cents for each bath."

Hardy stared. "Fifteen cents?"

"That includes the soap and a towel."

Hardy smiled. "Okay. I'm a new employee at the general store. The Walker's will pay for this."

Barry, the barber, looked at him from head to toe and back up. "I understand, and that's fine." He threw the towel down next to the tub, dropped a big, knotty chunk of soap into the water, closed the curtain, and left the room.

Hardy strutted to the general store, clean as he could be, wearing all new clothes and loving his new jeans. Wayne and Wanda gave him a round of applause when he walked in.

At lunchtime in the café, Hardy told everyone nearby how happy he was with his new job and new jeans. After the meal, two men followed him to the store. He showed them the new clothes that arrived the previous Saturday and made his first sale. Both men bought jeans. One also purchased a shirt.

His first day on the job seemed long and tiresome, but Hardy felt good about the work and slept well that night. The next day, he walked into the store fifteen minutes before his starting time. He had already figured the Walker's to be early risers and thought he would get to work before they arrived. He hoped they'd be impressed when they walked in and found him already at work.

Like the day before, Wayne and Wanda talked and laughed while rearranging merchandise like rocking chairs and butter churns. They greeted him and told him how happy they were about his performance. Wayne walked toward the rear door and said, "Follow me, Hardy." Outside, they stopped at the outhouse, and Wayne explained how to move it to a new location.

Hardy stared. "Are you kidding? You want me to move this thing? I used it only a couple of times."

"Well, it needs to be done, and it's all part of the job. You'll find the shovel in the tool bin at the back of our building."

At five-thirty the following morning, Hardy walked into the barbershop for another bath. He would have to pay for this one himself, but after yesterday's chore, he couldn't stand the thought of having breakfast before a bath. While he scrubbed himself, he worried about what nasty task Wayne would give him today.

Hardy glanced at the big grandfather clock in the corner as he walked into the store two minutes before six o'clock. The Walkers seemed bright and cheerful like always, but they, too, glanced at the clock. Wayne dipped his head at him.

"Okay, Hardy, I guess you met Melvin?"

"Melvin?"

"Yeah, in the corral. He's a mule but thinks he's human. Throw a bale of hay over the fence and fill the water trough. In about half an hour, I want you to hitch Melvin to the wagon and go pick up a load of firewood. Ever drove a wagon?"

"No, but after plowing the ground with a pair of stubborn mules, I'm sure I can drive a wagon. Although, you might have to help me hitch him up the first time."

Hardy swept floors for a half-hour, then headed out with Melvin and the wagon to meet lumberjacks who sold firewood and lumber. The directions Wayne drew with a pencil told him to turn right at the first intersection. Hardy's mouth dropped open. This was the same road that brought him here on the buckboard less than a month ago. His heart fluttered. Could it be? If he turned left instead of right, would the road lead him to the train?

There it was, up ahead. Hardy recognized the road. Did he dare turn left? He grew excited as many thoughts flew through his mind. When Hardy told Seth he wanted to return to the real world, Seth told him, *"This is the real world. Your other world was not, and once you're here, you have no way to leave." How could that be possible?*

When Melvin reached the intersection, Hardy drew a long, ragged breath. "Haw," he yelled. The mule stopped, snorted, and jerked his head to the right. Hardy yelled the command again and yanked the left rein. The mule turned the wagon left. Hardy's heart raced in his throat while he slapped the reins. "Giddyap."

Once more, the mule stopped and snorted. His long ears laid back against his head. Hardy ignored him, slapped the reins hard and yelled, "Giddyap, Melvin."

The beast pulled the wagon at a slow walk. "You can be as mule-headed as you want," Hardy chuckled, "but I'm the driver." He slapped the reins hard and yelled louder. Melvin took off at a trot.

Hardy's breath quickened again when he saw familiar markers, an odd-shaped tree, and a small pond on the roadside. He stood in the wagon to see farther ahead, but the jolting sat him sat him back down. again. A fuzzy image came into view in the distance. He wanted it to be a barn.

As the wagon grew closer, he tried once more to stand. Tears came. Yes, it was a barn, the same one he saw on the side of the road when he left the train. The railroad track would be close by and should soon be coming into view.

A sudden gust of wind blew in from the right side of the wagon. A bolt of lightning seared across the darkening sky and struck the ground a few yards in front of the mule. A thundering boom rattled the wagon.

Hardy caught a glimpse of the train in the distance ahead. But the mule bolted, made a sudden left turn across the field, and headed for the barn. Hardy screamed, "Whoa! whoa!" and yanked the reins.

The wagon rocked side-to-side. Hardy dropped the reins, grabbed onto the sideboard of the wagon, and jumped overboard. He landed with a thud that knocked his breath out of him while cold rain came down in sheets.

After long minutes, Hardy stirred. The rain ended after it soaked his clothes. He sat up and breathed deep, trying to regain his energy. Everything ached when he tried to move. Nothing seemed broken.

He looked around but saw no sign of the mule or wagon. He covered his face with his hands, wagged his aching head, and yelled, "Oh, Hardy! What have you done?"

Chapter Eleven

Hardy dragged himself off the ground, rubbed his aching legs, arms, and shoulders, and wished he could rub his aching back. Everything hurt. He drew a long, deep breath, knowing his pride hurt most of all.

He pushed himself up and tried to stand but lost his balance. On his third try, he spread his arms for balance and kept his feet farther apart to remain standing. After a few seconds, he braved a step. He wobbled a bit but stayed upright. With short, careful steps, Hardy walked toward the barn. Stopping to rest, he turned to look at the train. He drew a ragged breath. The train had gone. *Was it ever really there?*

He studied the barn and hoped it would not disappear before he got there. After ten minutes of slow walking, he stepped into the barn and let go a big sigh of relief. The mule had pulled the wagon into the barn and now munched hay near a stall. The wagon would need repairs, but nothing major.

In less than a half-hour, Hardy, Melvin, and the wagon headed for firewood. He focused on the two lumberjacks who cut and sold firewood. Both were big men, one about as tall as Hardy, the other perhaps three inches taller. The taller one, built like an oak tree, had an easy laugh that came often while he worked. With his short beard and bulging muscles, he reminded Hardy of Paul Bunyan, a character from a story he read many years ago. Hardy helped the men load the wagon, but they were much stronger and faster and did most of the work.

Three hours later, Hardy drove the loaded wagon toward the general store while thoughts about the morning plagued him. The mule tried to warn him when he turned left instead of right.

Did Melvin sense something dangerous? What caused the sudden storm? When he had limped into that huge barn in his wet overalls, he knew the weather was real. But the train? Did his mind play a trick on him?

Maybe Seth was right. He could never leave here. Yet Seth could leave whenever he wanted. He sat up straight and clutched the reins while Melvin pulled the wagon into the yard behind the general store. Wayne came out to greet them.

"Glad to see you made it home." He checked the wood stacked in the wagon and nodded. "Looks good. We've been running short for more than a week. The trip took longer than expected, and I've been a bit concerned."

Wayne walked around the wagon while he grabbed and shook damaged wall supports. He stopped next to Hardy and motioned at the damage. "What happened here? Did the lumberjacks get a little too rough loading the wagon? Or did you run into something?"

Hardy stepped out of the wagon and wiped his face with his bandanna. "I ran into rain, a *heavy* rain with a high wind. The mule got a little wild. I fell off the wagon, and he ran away. Took me quite a while to catch up to him and to get us back on the road."

Wayne nodded. "Looks like you and the mule are okay, and we can fix the wagon tomorrow." He unhitched the mule, put him in the corral, fed him, and went inside the store.

For more than an hour, Hardy unloaded firewood and stacked it in a shed by the fence. The job made him appreciate how hard the local people work to cook food and heat their homes. He stood straight and pressed his thumbs into the muscles of his lower back to ease the strain. He glanced at the nearby outhouse, grateful that today's job had been easier to handle than yesterdays.

Wayne walked out and nodded at the wagon. "I've brought many loads of firewood in that wagon, so I know how much work it is. Leave the wagon where it is, and we'll repair it tomorrow." He stared up at Hardy. "And tomorrow … I'll have a couple more questions about what happened on today's trip."

***

Hardy walked through Graham's Grocery Market trying to decide what to make for his dinner, or *supper* as the locals often called it. He tried to convince himself to cook his meals at home. But the merchandise here in the store highlighted many stark differences from his previous life. He would often throw a frozen meal in the microwave for five minutes and place the meal on the table. *Dinner is served.*

Now, he shopped for different types and cuts of meat, along with a variety of vegetables. He'd have to build a fire in his wood-burning stove, prepare and cook each item separately, and have a lot of cleanup afterward.

Hardy asked the store clerk where he could find the bread. The man offered a puzzled smile. "You'll find the sacks of flour and cornmeal in the aisle at the far wall, and baking powder is across the aisle from that. If you need milk, it's in the icebox over in the corner."

Hardy glanced at the clock in the corner of the store. The local café would be open for another forty-five minutes, and he could buy his meals on credit till payday. He nodded as he left the store. *Problem solved.*

After the meal and a short walk home, Hardy cleaned his room and turned in early. He hoped for a long, peaceful sleep. Instead, Wayne's last words woke Hardy several times during the night. What did his boss want to know about the trip, the mule, or the wagon?

Without enough sleep, he might wake up late. The Walkers would not put up with that. Yet, he had no alarm clock.

Tomorrow he would ask if Wayne or Wanda would stop by his room each morning and tap on the door to make sure he would not be late for work. With that solution in mind, he drifted off to sleep.

Hardy jerked awake, sat up, and looked through the window. A streak of sunshine above the horizon told him the day had begun. When he opened the store door, the big clock showed 4:45, plenty of time for breakfast at the café.

Hardy arrived at the store fifteen minutes early for his job. He said good morning to Wanda and heard hammering behind the store. Through the rear window, he saw Wayne installing new supports on the wagon walls.

Hardy walked out. "Good morning, Wayne. Another beautiful day isn't it."

"Indeed it is, Hardy. Good morning to you, too." He jerked his thumb toward the shed behind him. "Grab the other hammer and the wood chisel."

Over the next two-and-a-half hours, Wayne, and Hardy chiseled notches, cut supports and wall boards with a handsaw, and nailed them into place. While they worked, Wayne mentioned nothing about the time or cost to repair the wagon or about yesterday's trip.

Hardy could not believe Wayne would forget about all of it. And yet, for the rest of the day, Wayne said nothing about the trip while Hardy cleaned and stocked the higher shelves and watched Wayne help three customers who bought jeans and shirts to go with them.

Ten minutes before closing, Hardy took a big, cool drink from the water bucket. He replaced the dipper and turned to find Wayne sitting on a bench, with Wanda standing behind him. Wayne motioned for Hardy to sit.

Hardy sat across from him and chewed his bottom lip, expecting a lecture, or something worse, about yesterday's trip.

Wayne stood. "I know it's after hours, but I need a favor. I'd like you to throw about a hundred sticks of firewood into the wagon, hitch up Melvin, and follow us home. We'll unload the wagon, and you can drive it back."

Hardy hesitated. He had no food in his room, and the café would likely close before he got home. "Okay ... I'll start loading the firewood."

Wanda stepped beside Wayne. "Hardy, there's one more thing we'd like you to do tonight. Come and have supper with us. I'll start cooking as soon as we get home."

Hardy stood and grinned. "No way I could turn that down."

In the wagon, Hardy held the reins. Melvin followed the carriage. The mule often traveled this road through the woods and knew it well. Melvin would also know the way to the store and would pull the wagon at his own pace. Hardy would have to do nothing but ride. His mind felt at ease. Wayne still had said nothing about yesterday's trip. Hardy couldn't believe the man had forgotten about it.

***

Hardy's appetite seemed to have no limits, and the light conversation during supper did not slow him down. After he finished two large pork chops, he started to say, *Wow, I really pigged out.* But if the Walkers were unfamiliar with that phrase, they might misinterpret it.

"Thank you both very much. That was a great meal."

Wayne moved his chair away from the table. "You're welcome, Hardy. We're glad you came. We're also glad you decided to move from that other world to this one. I don't know much about that other world, but..." he angled his head at his wife..."over the years, Wanda and I have hired two other people from there. Neither stayed on the job very long. One was determined to go back where he came from, though his ambassador told him it couldn't be done."

The room grew quiet. Hardy assumed Wayne expected him to respond. He preferred to listen and waited for Wayne to continue.

Wayne sat up in his chair and folded his hands. "After that young man worked for us a few days, I sent him out with the wagon to pick up a load of lumber. A few hours after, he returned in a beat-up, empty wagon and told me a wild story about wind, heavy rains, thunder, and lightning and how Melvin went crazy. He blamed it all on the mule."

Wayne stood and turned to the water bucket in the corner. After a big drink, he returned the dipper to the bucket. He looked at his guest. "Hardy, anything more you'd like to tell us about your trip yesterday?" He returned to his chair.

Hardy stroked the lump in his throat and stood. "I'm sorry, Wayne." He turned to the lady of the house. "I apologize to you, too, Wanda."

He faced Wayne. "I did not leave the store with a plan to escape. But when I got to the first turn, I recognized the road and wanted to turn left to see if the train would be there a few miles down." He hoped Wayne or Wanda would speak, but they watched him and waited.

Hardy spread his hands. "I'm sorry I forced the mule to turn left instead of right. I made the wrong decision. The thunder, lightning, and heavy rain scared me. It was all real, and when Melvin took off for the barn, the wagon zigzagged like crazy. Luckily, I didn't kill myself when I jumped out."

Wayne nodded. "You are indeed lucky. So, if you had it to do over, would you go left or right?"

Hardy sat again. "If I had not made that mistake, I wouldn't have learned from it. Without that experience, I would probably do the same thing. But I learn from my mistakes. The

76

next time you give me directions, I will follow them. That's a promise. I did not lie about anything. I simply left out part of the truth."

On the way home, Melvin made all the decisions. Hardy had time to think about what happened tonight. He believed the Walkers trusted him more than before. He made a solemn promise to them—and to himself—to tell the truth from now on.

Before he left their home, Hardy asked the Walkers to knock on his door each morning to help him wake up on time.

Wanda smiled. "I think we can fix that." She brought a small box from another room and handed it to him. "Put this in the wagon's glovebox and open it when you get home. It's not a gift, but you can borrow it until we need it."

Hardy felt his face flush.as he looked at her. "If this is something you're gonna miss, maybe you should keep it here."

Wanda smiled and nodded. "If we need to see it, we can look at a drawing my sister made of it many years ago. Take good care of it. We'll let you know when we need it."

***

Hardy stared at the glovebox on the inside wall next to him. He took out the box Wanda gave him and said aloud, "Why should I wait?"

He hoped he would find an alarm clock. What else would solve his problem? But driving through the woods in the dark, he could not see what he held in his hand. When the woods thinned, the clock glistened in the moonlight between the trees. Hardy saw a beautiful windup alarm clock with large hands and large numbers on the dial and twin alarm bells on top. A lump grew in his throat. It resembled the clock that mesmerized him at his great-grandmother's home on his seventh birthday. He had always treasured that memory of his great-grandmother, a special lady who loved him dearly. Today, Hardy felt guilty. He could not recall her name.

With Melvin and the wagon in place, Hardy grabbed a candle from his room, took his clock downstairs, and set the time to match the store clock.

With his new treasure on the wall shelf above the bed, Hardy would sleep well that night with a full belly and no worries about sleeping late. The clock meant much more than knowing the time of day or not being late for work. The clock proved the Walkers trusted him. No one could put a price on that.

Besides, they didn't need an alarm anyway. Their wacky backyard rooster took care of that job.

Chapter Twelve

On Sunday morning, Hardy woke at 7:30, the latest he'd slept since arriving in Mystique. He didn't know if anyone expected to see him at church today. But while he put on his favorite shirt and a pair of jeans, he knew it didn't matter. He'd make up his own mind about Sundays.

Today, Hardy would celebrate his first anniversary. Yet it seemed impossible. He'd been here in Mystique for one full year. In this country, if this place *is* a country. In this time zone, wherever it was. That alone seemed impossible.

Many memories of his past life and people he once knew had disappeared somewhere into the far reaches of his mind. How many? He had no way to know.

Hardy brought home a bacon-egg-biscuit from the café last night for breakfast this morning. He grabbed the wrapped biscuit from the cupboard and slid it into his shirt pocket. He wrapped his bandanna around a pint jar of water and tied the bandanna to his belt. Grabbing his hat, he stepped out, locked the door, and hurried down the stairs.

He could not remember the last time he went for a walk to get away and clear his mind. He could recall someone, probably his father, who believed the easiest way to solve a problem was to leave it behind and look back at it. *You get a whole new perspective*, he would say.

Hardy had no problems today. A good time to do what he wanted. His steps came light and easy. Maybe, just *maybe*, his life was heading in the right direction.

He'd found the Walkers great people to work for and work with, and they promised a pay hike when he finished one year on the job. That day would be here soon.

Minutes later, Hardy crossed a short, wooden bridge that spanned a narrow, fast-moving stream, its bottom lined with large stones. He wondered why he had not noticed that bridge before. It might look different from a wagon or while sitting on a horse.

He turned right off the road and walked along the bank. Birds chirped in the trees. Squirrels rustled through the leaves, digging up acorns and scratching for food. A chipmunk scurried toward its burrow.

The creek grew wider. Hardy walked and watched the water ripple over the stones. After several minutes more, he glanced at the sun and guessed he had walked about two miles. Time for a short break, he told himself and sat on a stump left by a woodcutter.

After a long drink from his water jar, Hardy's stomach made demanding noises. He unwrapped the biscuit and made his stomach happy while he listened to the faint swishing and scratching of wildlife around him in the sparse, quiet forest.

Rested and ready for more exploring, he stood when he heard a faint call from farther downstream. He walked a few steps and stopped to listen. It came again, like someone calling for help. He walked fast downstream, stopped, and cupped his ear. He heard another desperate call for help.

Hardy stood tall. "Hello. Where are you?" No answer. He moved fast while listening to the sound but heard only the rapids.

Now he ran, jumping over stones and brush. He stopped once more, cupped his mouth, and yelled, "Hello, where are you?" Still, he heard nothing but rapids. In a dead run, Hardy strained his lungs as he called out but got no reply.

A flash of reality told Hardy a person in the rapids would hear nothing except the noise of the water around him.

He ran faster but tripped over a large stone and fell. He scrambled to his feet and felt something warm on his face. He wiped it and discovered a bloody nose.

He refused to quit. The creek grew wider. The sound of rushing water grew louder. He could see the rapids now, but the sunlight made brilliant sparkles on the water, forcing him to shade his eyes and look away.

Hardy stared at the ground and rested his eyes. A minute later, he raised his head with slow, easy moves to let his eyes adjust. He looked up again, his eyes half-closed, and strained his vision. His breath caught. Across the creek, a shivering child held onto a long tree root that grew out into the water.

The child held the root with one hand, his other hand hanging by his side. The lad faced the opposite bank, and Hardy had no way to get his attention. He called out but assumed the child on the other side of the creek would never hear him above the roar.

A lump grew in Hardy's throat. He had to rescue that little boy but found no bridge, no log across the creek, no shallow area without dangerous, slippery stones where he could wade across.

He kept running, searching, hoping to find something that would help. Anything at all. Farther downstream on Hardy's side of the creek, a giant tree stood near the bank, and a large limb hung over the water.

"I may be crazy," he said aloud while he ran toward the tree, "but it's all I've got."

Under the tree, he leaped, trying to catch a low-hanging branch but missed. He fell to his knees, jumped up, backed off, and ran to try once more, yelling, "Please, God." His feet left the ground.

Hardy caught the smaller branch and pulled himself up. He climbed higher to reach the huge limb hanging over the water and worked toward the opposite bank.

Hardy turned on the branch to see the child in the water below him. The boy still held the giant root with one hand, shivering. Hardy knew the young boy's waning strength could not hold him in place much longer.

With the child turned away from him, Hardy would not call out. The boy had little chance of hearing him. If the boy did hear the call, he might let go of the root and turn to see who came to save him. That could be a disaster.

Smaller branches near the end of the limb began to bend and shake as Hardy edged farther out. The risk played in his mind. *If a branch breaks when I step on it, I'll fall, maybe head-first.* He glanced down at the large rocks not far below the water's surface.

The young lad shivered much harder. Hardy knew the poor child could not hang on to the wet root much longer.

The boy cried aloud, "Somebody help me. Please."

A myriad of emotions flashed through Hardy's mind. Fear. Courage. Compassion. Responsibility.

He had no time to wait, no time to plan. He would risk everything to save the life of a child.

He stepped on a small branch that bent beneath his weight. Hardy took a deep breath, let go of the branch above, and spread his arms for balance. Two seconds seemed a long time before his boots struck the water behind the boy.

Hardy screamed, "Hang on!"

The child did not hang on, but turned toward Hardy, reached out his right hand, and grabbed his rescuer's arm. The boy missed and fell forward.

Hardy lunged toward him and caught him as he fell. He kept the lad from striking the large rocks with his head, but man and child now struggled face down in the fast-moving stream. Hardy pushed up and tried to stand.

He slipped, lost his balance, and fell, his knees hitting the rocks. Jerking his head side to side, he saw the lad roll over, face up. The boy's hat left his head and floated downstream ahead of him. His hair, once stuffed beneath the hat, now covered the boy's shoulders in the water. The child paddled with one hand, maybe unaware he headed for the rapids. Or had he given up?

Hardy planted his foot against a huge rock on the bottom of the creek, turned toward the lad, and pushed off with all his strength. He caught the boy's foot, hoping the shoe would not come off while he pulled the boy toward him. He caught the child around the waist and pulled him to his feet.

While the boy's left arm hung limp at his side, his right hand grabbed Hardy's wrist. His eyes pleaded. He tried to speak, but only grunts came from his open mouth.

"Get on my back," Hardy yelled and tried to turn his back to the boy. The grip grew tighter on Hardy's wrist as the boy shook his head.

Hardy squeezed the little wrist until the child let go. Hardy yelled, "Get on my back!" While the kid fought him, Hardy held the child's wrist and turned his back to him. "Get on my back!" he yelled again. "Help me here before we both drown."

The boy did not speak. Tears ran down his face, but he nodded, still shivering. Hardy made a slow turn and stooped to help the child, knowing it would be a tough task for the boy who could not use his left arm.

The child moaned, struggled, and cried but got high enough on Hardy's back for Hardy to hang on to him. The creek bank lay about 20 feet away, but getting there would be tough with water rushing over the stones.

With each step, Hardy planted his feet on a solid rock. If he slipped with the boy on his back, the fall could be deadly for both. While he struggled toward the bank, the lad grunted and moaned with each step.

A large rock at the edge of the bank offered the steppingstone Hardy had hoped for. Would it be sturdy enough? If it moved when he stepped up, he and the boy would likely crash onto the rocks at the bottom. Such a fall could be deadly for both.

The child on his back made no more sound, but Hardy felt him shivering from the cold water. When a shuddered wracked the small body, he knew the child was still crying. This poor little boy had been through so much in a short time. A lump grew in Hardy's throat as he planted his foot on the rock and pushed.

The rock did not move. That did not guarantee the next rock would stay in place. A rare recollection of his father flashed in his mind. Hardy heard his Dad's words from years ago. *Nothing worth doing comes without risk.*

Hardy set his foot on the rock, reached back with the opposite foot, took a deep breath, and pushed forward with more energy than he'd ever known. With another long step up, Hardy and his new friend landed on solid ground.

The long hair brushed Hardy's shoulders and back while he stepped up on the bank of the creek.

***

Breathing heavy, Hardy and the child sat facing each other. Neither spoke, but Hardy smiled. Tears ran down the child's face, and he turned and looked away.

With a slow, calm voice, Hardy said, "I think we're okay now, young man. My name is Hardy. What's your name?"

The child turned farther away and did not speak. Hardy stared at the ground. *Is this boy too shy to talk? Is he afraid of me? Is he lost? A runaway? Could this child be deaf?* Hardy's heart went out to him.

He watched the child's curly, shoulder-length, red hair soak his already-wet shirt as the hair dried in the fading sunlight between the trees.

Hardy cleared his throat. "Your shirt will dry faster if you take it off and hang it on a limb."

The child swung around and faced him. "I will not take off my shirt."

Hardy sat up straight. "Sorry, just trying to help."

The child leaned forward and stared at him. "My name is Debra."

Chapter Thirteen

Hardy stared in disbelief. "Are you telling me you're a…girl?"

Debra stared back at him. "Are you telling me I look like a *boy*?"

"No, no. It's just that, uhh…your long hair was stuffed under your hat and…" He sighed. "You're wearing jeans and…"

Debra shrugged. "Girls can wear whatever they want."

"Yes, I know. I'm sorry I mistook you for a boy. How old are you, Debra?"

"Why do you want to know that?" She sat up straight and raised her chin. "How old are *you*? Is that okay to ask?"

Hardy smiled and nodded. "I don't mind at all. I'm twenty-two."

"You're a lot older than me. I'm eleven." She looked down and shook her head. "Please don't hurt me, Mister Hardy."

"Oh, Debra, I would never hurt you. I'm trying to help you. Why did you come out here alone? That doesn't seem like a safe thing to do."

She took a deep breath and let it go. "I wanted to go for a walk by myself, but…I got lost." She wiped a tear from her cheek and pointed at the tree behind Hardy.

"I climbed up there to look for my house, any house, a barn, or a trail, but I couldn't see anything. Only trees. And then I fell." She wiped at another tear.

"When I first saw you in the water, I noticed you didn't use your left arm. Anything I can do to help? Is it hurting?"

Debra raised her arm a bit and stared at it. "It's better. I guess I have to wait for it to heal up."

Hardy stood and leaned toward her. "Did you fall on it?"

She nodded and pointed to the limb above him. "I was on that limb and started to come down, but my foot slipped, and I fell in the water. I almost couldn't get up, but finally, I did, and I grabbed onto that part of the tree in the water. I was there for a long time, crying and yelling for help. Then you came and helped me. Thank you, Mister Hardy."

"You are very welcome, Debra. You're lucky to be alive, young lady. Falling that far on those rocks could have killed you." Hardy stepped closer and stopped. "It's gonna be dark in an hour, maybe less. Do you live nearby, or is your home a long way?"

She turned up her palms. "I think it's a long way, but I don't know which way it is. I walked around in circles when I got lost."

"Debra, I want to help you get home, but I have no idea where to start. Which way do we go from here?"

She stared. "I don't know."

"Did you cross the creek anywhere? Did you see a bridge?"

Her mouth dropped open while she shook her head. "No."

Hardy turned and looked at the tree. "Okay, stay where you are, and see if you can help me when I climb up there. I'll tell you what I see, and you tell me if you recognize anything." He climbed to the second big limb, looked around, and called down to her. "I don't see any houses or barns."

Back on the ground, he stood in front of her. "Do you live in Mystique?"

"No. We live out in the country."

"Where do you go to school?"

"The same school as all the other kids."

"In Mystique? You go to the school by the church?"

"That's the only one I know."

"Okay, now we're getting somewhere."

Her eyes brightened. "Do you live in Mystique?"

"Yes, I work at the General Store, and I can get us there." He looked up at the sky. "But it's at least a two-hour walk, and I won't risk it in the dark."

To prepare for the night, Hardy scooped leaves into a big pile next to a tree and turned to Debra. "We'll have to wait till morning. When you're ready to go to sleep, lay down on the leaves and get comfortable. I'll cover you with a lot more leaves to keep you warm during the night." He motioned at a nearby tree. "I'll be right by that tree if you need me."

She looked up at him. "Thank you for being so nice. You don't have to be so nice to me, because I did a bad thing."

"I don't think you did anything bad. I'll help you any way I can. When we get you home, I'll tell your parents how good you've been."

She frowned. "Do you have anything to eat? I'm so hungry."

Hardy drew in a deep breath. "So sorry, I brought a sandwich, but I ate that early today before I heard you calling. Before we take off for home tomorrow morning, I'll see what I can do."

She bit her lip. Pleading eyes looked up at him. "I'm so scared."

He took her hand. "Everything will be okay. Lay down and get comfortable. I'll cover you with more leaves."

Long minutes later, Hardy lay down under his own leaf pile a few feet from Debra. He worried about her as she sniffled, and cried herself to sleep. He fell asleep after light snoring came from the other leaf bed.

Within minutes, an owl woke him with endless hoots Soon after, he heard movement and rustling leaves. . He did not move when a shivering young girl snuggled up against his back.

Something about that seemed very wrong. Yet, an 11-year-old child…lost, cold, hungry, and afraid … needed a rescue. In the morning, he would try to find some mushrooms for her breakfast.

When he heard her soft snores behind him, Hardy slept again.

***

Still half-asleep, Hardy stirred at a *clump, clump* sound, like soft hoofbeats of a horse. With little rest during the night, his exhausted body and frazzled mind would not allow a silly dream to interrupt his sleep. Hardy dozed off once more at the soft sound of a child's breath behind him.

A short time after, he jerked awake when a deep voice above him yelled, "Hey, Jody, over here! I think I found her."

Debra screamed and jumped up. Hardy jumped up after her, out of breath, his heart racing. A man with a rifle stood beside him.

Hardy stammered, "Are you … uhh … Debra's father?"

A man with a shotgun appeared on Hardy's other side. "No, he's not. But *I* am." His face distorted. "Get away from my daughter, you filthy maggot. I ought a fill your belly full of buckshot. Right here, and right now."

Debra screamed again, reached up, and grabbed her daddy's waist. "Oh, Daddy, Daddy, hug me, please. I love you so much."

Hardy raised his arms high while the man held the gun in one hand. Daughter and father hugged and cried. "I love you, Daddy," Debra said.

"I love you too, my sweet baby… are you all right?"

The other man waved at her. "Debra, are you okay? We're so happy to find you."

Debra turned toward him. "Yes, Uncle Luther. Thank you for finding me."

Hardy shivered, his arms growing tired from holding up his hands. "Hey, guys, I can explain…."

Luther slapped him and shouted, "Shut up. We don't wanna hear it."

From his saddlebag, Debra's father pulled a coil of rope and tossed it to his brother. "Here you go, Luther. You know what to do with this."

Hardy's breath caught in his throat. "Hey, I…"

Luther leveled his rifle at Hardy. "If you don't close that lying hole in your face, I'm gonna put a bullet in it."

Luther pulled a monster of a knife from his saddlebag and wiggled the huge blade under Hardy's nose. "Turn around. Put your hands behind you, and don't even breathe till I tell you."

Hardy turned and crossed his wrists behind him. Luther cut a length of rope and tied Hardy's hands.

Jody led his horse into a clearing while his daughter followed. He mounted and helped her up behind him. She leaned forward. "Daddy, I'm so hungry."

90

Jody handed her a sandwich from the saddlebag. She took a big bite and wiped her mouth with her hand. "Thank you. I love you, Daddy. Is Uncle Luther going with us?"

Jody leaned toward his brother and yelled, "Hey, Luther, when we leave here, make a fast ride into town, and let everybody know we rescued my daughter. Debra and I will be there in a couple of hours." He pointed his shotgun at Hardy. "With that monster in front of us."

"I'll ride over to Mayor Miller's place and tell him," Luther said. Then I'll ride into town and announce it at the café."

Jody held up his hand and gave Luther the *okay* sign.

Luther frowned as he looked at the piles of leaves near the tree, then at Hardy. "Is that what I think it is?"

Hardy leaned toward the man. "You got it all wrong. I never…"

Luther leveled his gun at him. "Shut up. I don't want to hear your lies. You are one filthy excuse for a human. Do you have any idea how old that little girl is?"

He backhanded Hardy across the face. "Turn around and put your forehead against that tree. If you move while I'm searching you, I'll have to dig a grave out here in the woods."

After the search, the man held up two quarters. "Is this all the money you got?"

Hardy replied with his head still against the tree, though his swollen lip made some words hard to pronounce. "If it's two quarters, it's all I have."

Luther dragged out his words. "Okay… turn around… slow … and easy."

Hardy's aching back brought tears to his eyes when he turned.

Luther snickered. "Okay, you filthy weasel, walk over there and stop in front of my brother's horse." He snatched up his rifle and shook it in Hardy's face. "You see this little baby? I can shoot a chigger off a chipmunk from 40 yards out. If you get out of line … I'll prove it to you."

Chapter Fourteen

Hardy walked along the edge of the creek with his hands tied behind him. Jody followed on his horse. Twice, when Debra spoke up and tried to tell her father what happened, he told her to keep quiet. "This is the wrong time for you to say anything about what happened, my dear."

When they reached the road that led to town, Hardy stumbled on the bridge and fell to his knees. Jody stopped his horse near him and dismounted. "If you're trying to trick me, young man, it won't work." He caught his prisoner's elbows and pulled him up while Hardy moaned with pain.

Debra cried out, "Please, Daddy, don't—"

Jody spun around. "Quiet. I'll let you know when to talk." He turned back to Hardy.

Tears came to Debra's eyes. Her face full of anger and pity, she took the half-eaten sandwich from the saddle bag and tossed it to the ground behind her.

With a raspy voice, Hardy turned to face Jody. "Could I have some … water … please?" He angled his head at the bottle fastened to his belt.

Debra jumped down from the horse. "I'll help him, Daddy."

Jody glared. "No, you won't. He can wait till we get into town."

Debra sobbed as she and Jody remounted.

Long minutes dragged by before the group reached the edge of town on their way to the meetinghouse behind the school. Like a holiday crowd at a parade, people came out of homes and businesses to watch while Hardy, Jody, and Debra passed by.

Hardy held his head high. As the leader of this parade, he had no reason to be ashamed. *Ironic*, he told himself. *The last person in this parade also knows I'm innocent. But, if Luther had done the brainwashing job Jody wanted, the townspeople would likely decide I'm guilty of something horrible.* He wondered if Maxwell Miller believed the story from Luther. Hardy assumed Seth had heard the story by now if he was anywhere around the town. Hardy knew he could count on Seth. The man seemed too smart and informed to buy that kind of trash from anyone here.

Outside the homes, offices, and businesses, people stood and gawked while Hardy struggled to keep a positive attitude. But his breath caught, his heart pounded, and he felt the warm color on his face when he saw Wayne and Wanda in a small crowd outside the General Store. The Walkers stood, mouths open, and watched the parade along with everyone else.

Hardy turned his head to face them and tried to force a smile. When a tear ran down his cheek, he assumed his smile had failed.

***

An hour later, inside the meeting hall, Mayor Miller gave Hardy a dipper of cool water. With his hands tied in front of him, Hardy faced a small crowd. He knew Maxwell Miller as a fair and reasonable man with common sense, but Hardy had hoped the Walkers would show up here, at least one of them. More than anyone else, he wanted to see Seth.

The mayor rapped a gavel. Everyone stood, though Hardy was the last to make it to his feet. "This hearing is now in session," the mayor declared. He turned and looked at Hardy. "Mister Hardy Brooke … is that your proper name?"

"Yes, sir."

"The town of Mystique has called this inquiry to discuss a report that you were with an eleven-year-old girl. We have witnesses who said they found you with her in a wooded area near Mystique Creek. We are here to determine the details of that situation."

He rapped his gavel. "Everyone, please be seated."

"Mister Jody Watts. Do you have a complaint against this man in the defendant's chair?"

Jody stood. "I do, Mister Mayor. My eleven-year-old daughter disappeared early yesterday morning. As you can imagine, her mother and I have been worried sick. We searched for her everywhere we could imagine and stayed up all night, praying she was okay. This morning my brother and I found her with that man." He pointed at Hardy. "They were lying next to each other on the ground when we found them, covered with leaves."

The mayor turned to Hardy. "How old are you, Mister Hardy Brooke?"

Hardy stood. "Twenty-two, sir." He sat again.

Jody Watts wiped his brow with his bandanna and stuck it back in his pocket. "My daughter is eleven years old. This man is twice her age. There is absolutely nothin' proper about the two of them laying together in the woods. Nobody would believe that was my daughter's idea. So, I don't want to hear that from anybody."

The mayor sat making notes while Jody talked. He stopped and looked up. "Mister Watts, can I assume you talked to your daughter about this incident? And if so, tell us what she said, please."

"No, Mister Mayor. I didn't have much time for that." He pulled out his pocket watch. "It's been maybe three hours and a half since we found her this morning." He pointed at Hardy. "I just wanted to get her away from that animal."

Hardy's face grew red as he stood. The mayor rapped his gavel. "Mister Brooke, you will rise only when directed to do so."

Hardy frowned and sat down. "Yes, sir."

The mayor scribbled another note and looked up. "Jody, we've known each other a long time, and I know you're a decent, honest man. But I have to ask you…any way you could be mistaken about this? I've known Mister Brooke for only a short time, but he made an impression on me as an honest, upright young man. I would like to talk with your daughter here in this room to hear her story."

Jody nodded. "I understand, Mister Mayor. I will talk to her this afternoon. Can we take this up tomorrow?"

The mayor ducked his head toward him. "I would like to hear from her today, with the incident still fresh in her mind. I prefer that you do not discuss it with her before she is here in the room with us." He rapped the gavel. "We will reconvene in one hour. Please bring your daughter here at that time."

Within minutes, two men re-tied Hardy's hands behind him and took him outside behind the building. They opened the door to a rundown shack a few yards away and steered Hardy inside.

Hardy wrinkled his nose and looked at them. "What is this? A jail?"

One man shook his head. "I've heard of real jails but never seen one. This one used to be a chicken coop, but they did a little bit of work on it and turned it into a lockup. Don't get used much, but it'll likely be your home for a few days."

"What do you mean, a few days? I didn't get charged with anything and didn't do anything wrong."

"It ain't up to us," the other replied. "But the outhouse is on the other side of that door. It's built-on, so whoever is in here can't get away."

Hardy glared. "You can't do this. I have not been charged with anything. I've done nothing wrong. I've had nothing to eat since yesterday morning, and my hands are still tied."

"Well, the café is open. We can bring some food. You got any money?"

"No. I had two quarters in my pocket this morning. But that guy, Luther, stole them when he searched me. He never gave them back."

The man's eyes grew wide. "Well, looks like nothing we can do."

"Oh yes, there is," Hardy told him. "Mayor Miller is a friend of mine. Ask him to come see me, please."

One of the men chuckled. "I don't think that's gonna happen." He untied Hardy's hands and nodded at him. "But I'll tell him."

***

After an hour that seemed like a day, the two men returned to the chicken coop lockup and took Hardy to the meeting room. Again, they tied his hands in front of him and led him to his chair up front.

Jody Watts sat in the same chair as before with Debra beside him. Instead of jeans, she wore a colorful dress and new shoes. Hardy wanted to make eye contact with her but assumed someone told her, *don't look at him.*

With the meeting once more in order, the mayor asked Debra Watts to stand.

"Hello, Debra. I've seen you a few times before, and you've grown a lot lately."

She blushed but did not respond. The mayor leaned in his chair toward her. "Do you remember me, Debra?"

Debra shrugged. Her face grew red. She did not answer.

"Debra, do you know why we are here?"

She shook her head.

The mayor turned up his palms and motioned to her. "I want you to know you are not in any trouble. We need you to tell us what happened in the last two days. Look at the man here in this chair." He motioned at Hardy. "And tell us if you know him."

She turned her head toward Hardy and nodded yes.

"Thank you, Debra. Tell us the last time you saw him, please."

Debra glanced at Jody, and then remained silent.

The mayor waited. "Was it this morning?" Debra stared at the floor.

The mayor stood. "Okay, Debra. You may sit down now. We're not making much progress." He scanned the audience, then looked at Jody. "Mister Watts, is your wife here?"

Jody stood. "No, Mister Mayor. She's at home with our nine-year-old son."

"I am going to recess this hearing and would like to reconvene tomorrow morning at 9 AM. Would you please ask your wife to attend along with Debra at that time? If you would like, you can stay home with your son."

"Okay, Mister Mayor."

The mayor rapped the gavel, and people started filing out of the building. Hardy jumped up from his chair. "Mayor Miller, any way I could talk to you for a couple of minutes?"

The mayor looked at him. "At this point, I cannot discuss the hearing with you in private."

"It's not about the hearing, sir."

"Okay, I'm going to the café. After I finish my meal, I'll come over to the lockup and talk to you."

"Could you bring me some food, sir? I've had nothing to eat since yesterday morning."

***

Within a half-hour, Mayor Miller stopped at the lockup door with one of the guards. As they stepped inside, the mayor placed a full plate of food on a small table in the corner. Hardy's mouth watered. He scrubbed his hands in a wash pan, grabbed a wooden crate for a chair, and looked for a fork.

"Sorry, I forgot to bring you some tools to eat with," the mayor said.

Hardy smiled. "Not a problem." He wiped his hands on his shirt and grabbed a chicken leg.

The mayor chuckled. "That may not work well for the mashed potatoes and gravy. I'll be right back."

Keeping his promise, the mayor handed Hardy a fork. He wolfed down the plate of food in under ten minutes. When he finished, the mayor looked at him. "Now, Hardy, Is there anything you would like to say to me?"

"Sorry, I can't pay you right now, sir. When those men first saw me out in the woods, Luther searched me and stole two quarters from my pocket. That's all I had, and he kept them. Thank you for the meal."

The mayor laughed. "You're welcome."

Hardy wiped his mouth on his sleeve. "You know me, sir. I won't escape. You don't need to keep me locked up in here. You helped me get that job at the General Store, and the Walkers need me. I may be awful at plowing ground but I can stock shelves and sell merchandise with the best of them. Let me go to work, and I'll come over for the hearing any time you say."

The mayor drew in a deep breath. "I'm sorry, Hardy. The claim being made against you is pretty serious, and I need to hear from little Debra before I make a decision on that."

"I understand, sir. But I promise you I will be there. It's the only way I could ever get cleared of this."

"I understand Hardy. But I'll have to wait for some worthwhile testimony, one way or the other."

Chapter Fifteen

Hardy woke often during the night, convinced the dirty cot would work well as a torture device but never as a bed. Lying down worked little better than standing up. When his exhausted body finally surrendered to sleep, a loud rooster brought him awake.

He sat up, shaking his head, wondering if the rooster had found a way into the chicken coop with him. Then someone pounded on the door and yelled, "Mister Brooke, if you need the outhouse, better do it now. We gotta take you to the meeting house."

Hardy rubbed his swollen face. "What? Now? What time is it?"

"Ten minutes before 9 o'clock. We'll give you five minutes."

Ten minutes later, Hardy sat in the same chair. the Watts having filed a formal charge against Hardy for unbecoming and indecent actions in the presence of their daughter."

"Is that accurate, Mr. and Mrs. Watts?" the mayor asked.

They nodded and replied, "Yes, sir."

The mayor motioned at the five people seated behind him. "These honorable people have agreed to act as the jury."

Hardy sat with his head back, mouth open, his body shaking. The mayor turned toward him. "Stand and tell us how you plead, Mister Brooke."

Hardy jumped up out of his chair. "Absolutely not guilty, sir. Not one word of that is true." He pointed to Debra with his tied hands. "Tell them, Debra. Please tell them the truth."

The mayor rapped his gavel and yelled, "That's enough. You are never to speak directly to anyone else in this room without prior consent from me. Do you understand, Mister Brooke?"

Hardy held his hands toward him. "I'm addressing you now, Mister Mayor, and *here's* what I understand. People who did not see what happened when I rescued that little girl from the creek have falsely accused me. I have heard her say *nothing* against me because she knows I did nothing wrong."

He hung his head and shook it, then looked up at the mayor. "Why has no one in this room asked *me* what happened? I came along peacefully when those two men showed up in the forest because I expected justice. I have no one to speak for me, and this is the first time I've been allowed to speak for myself."

Hardy turned toward the crowd. "I've been in this town barely a year, and I've been told the people here have a high regard for justice. I accepted that as fact. But after what I've seen in the last two days, I no longer believe that."

He swept his head from side to side and nodded toward the audience. "If anyone here thinks he can prove me wrong about that, stand up and try."

Mayor Miller rapped the gavel and jumped to his feet. "Sit down, Mister Brooke. Any more speeches like that, and you will stay in lockup while we conduct this trial. Do you understand me?"

Hardy sat without responding. The mayor rapped his gavel. "We're going to break for a short recess. You may leave the room but return to your seats within fifteen minutes." He pulled his watch from his pocket. "You have until nine forty-five. I can't permit anyone into the room after that time. Please be quiet and courteous. Thank you." He caught the attention of the two guards and motioned them forward. He whispered to them, and they turned to Hardy and asked him to stand. They tied his hands behind him and led him back to lockup.

Hardy spent two minutes in the outhouse, then cleaned his hands in the wash pan. As he dried his hands, Mayor Miller walked in.

"Hardy, if you want to tell your side of the story, you're gonna have to behave in the meeting room."

"I meant no disrespect, sir but with no lawyers here in Mystique, I must defend myself. That's okay as long as I'm allowed to do that."

So far, I've not been treated fairly. Don't get me wrong, please. I don't mean *you* have been unfair, but the *system* here is unfair. No one talked to me about this before I got locked up. Why didn't someone ask me what happened out there in the forest with Debra? I would have told them everything. Then, they could ask Debra in private, not with her father around. I believe she would tell the exact same story I would tell."

"You will get a chance, Hardy. But I have to go through this procedure in the proper order and—"

"How can it be justice to accuse someone of a crime and charge him with it before he's allowed to tell his side of the story?" Hardy interrupted

"Hardy, I did not invent the procedures here nor how they are conducted. But as this goes forward, I will do my utmost to see that you get fair treatment. That's all I can do."

With the meeting back in order, Mayor Miller asked Debra's father to stand. "Jody Watts, did you question your daughter at home about all that happened while she was gone? If so, did she volunteer it, or did you have to coax her?"

"Well, Mister Mayor, she volunteered much of it. But some of it, I had to assume."

"Assume? What was that based on, Mister Watts? What did you assume?"

"I assumed that Mister Brooke had been out in the forest with my daughter the whole night. We found them early Monday morning, my brother, Luther, and me."

"Where did you find them, Mister Watts? Were they in a shelter of some kind? Out in the open? Under a tree?"

"Yes, sir." He nodded. "Under a tree."

Mayor Miller stood and extended his hand toward Debra's mother. "Mrs. Watts, I would like to ask you and Debra to have a seat on the bench out in front of our building for a few minutes. This time of the day, I think it's shaded out there. We will call you before long."

With Debra and her mother outside, the mayor sat and asked Luther Watts to stand. "Luther, we have heard that you were with your brother, Jody, when you found Debra out in the forest. Is that correct?"

"Yes, sir. I was there."

"After the incident, were you in Debra's presence at any time her father or mother talked to her about what happened out there?"

"Yes, at their home, I heard her tell my brother all about it."

"Thank you, Luther. Would you give us your general impression of the conversation? What did you conclude, and why?"

"Sir, more than anything else, it made me want to ask Mister. Hardy a few questions, especially here in this room. Jody and I discussed it, and he would like me to represent him since he is the one pressing charges. Is it okay if I do that now?"

"Well, Luther, it's not something we often do. That's not typical in hearings and trials. That's *my* job. But I will leave it up to Mister Hardy."

Hardy stood. "I have no problem with his questions, Mister Mayor. I have nothing to hide."

Luther strutted up the aisle, stopped in front of Hardy, crossed his arms, and tilted his head.

"Mister Brooke, how many times did you see Debra, the victim, before you got together with her in the woods?"

Hardy glared. "What? Victim? She's not a victim of anything. I don't remember seeing her before that unless it was at church."

"Really? I heard you tell somebody that you work at the General Store. So, is that not true?"

"I *do* work there, and the Walkers are great people."

"Debra says she's been in that store several times. But you're claiming you never saw her?"

"If so, I don't remember it. What's that got to do with anything?"

"Did you deal with her in the store?"

"No, I don't think so. I'd likely remember that."

Luther cocked his head. "And yet, you found a way to meet her in the woods. Or did the two of you just happened to show up there at the same place at the same *time*? Is that what you want us to believe?"

"I don't care what you believe," Hardy spat. "I did nothing wrong. Absolutely nothing. And I was respectful and very careful in dealing with Debra."

"Oh? Respectful? Careful? Isn't it true, that you asked her to take off her shirt after you two were done with your little swim in the creek?"

"You got it all wrong. I merely suggested that she take it off because…

"Merely suggested? Did she take it off?"

"No, she did not. At the time, I had no idea that she was a …."

"No idea? Are you going to tell us you thought pretty little Debra was a *boy*? You're not actually going to say that, are you?"

Hardy jumped to his feet and leaned forward. "She was wearing her brother's jeans, and her hair was stuffed up under a hat, and I—"

"And" Luther shouted, "You thought you would get her to undress while you pretended she was a boy. This topic gets more disgusting all the time. And so do *you*."

Mayor Miller rapped the gavel and got to his feet. "That is quite enough, Mister Watts. Take your seat." His gaze followed the man as he returned to his chair. "You have made me regret my previous decision, Luther."

He looked at Hardy. "And you may take *your* seat, Mister Brooke. Now, I would like to ask the Watts brothers to step outside the room for a few minutes while I talk to some other people here. Please ask Mrs. Watts and Debra to come in. I will send someone out to bring you in when we are done."

Luther stared. "But … Mayor Miller, I can sit here in the last row if you like, and I won't say a word."

The mayor glared at him. "The last row is filled, Mister Watts. Take a seat out front, and we will send for you in a few minutes. Mister Jody Watts, you will also have a seat on the bench outside with your brother. Someone will usher both of you back in as soon as it's time. Thank you."

Jody raised his hand. "Mayor Miller, I can wait right here"

The mayor picked up his gavel and pointed it at Jody. "Yes, you can, Mister Watts. But if you do not do what I ask, I will call this a mistrial. Then you can sit anywhere you like because all the rest of us will be going home, including the defendant." He nodded toward the door and motioned for one of Hardy's security guards to accompany the men outside.

When the door closed behind the Watts brothers, the Mayor sat and asked Debra's mother to stand.

"Mrs. Watts, did you discuss all of this with your daughter?"

"We talked about it."

The mayor extended his open hand toward Debra. "Debra, did you tell your mother everything that happened while you were gone?"

Debra stood but did not look at him. "No, sir."

"Mrs. Watts, tell us what you learned, please?"

Bonnie Watts nodded. "She was gone when we got up Sunday morning, and, of course, we panicked. We looked everywhere throughout our house, the barn, and the chicken house… everywhere. We kept calling her, and I was crying so hard. We wanted our darling girl back with us, and safe."

"I understand," the mayor interrupted, "please tell us what you and your daughter discussed after she came home."

With tears in her eyes, Bonnie turned, looked at her daughter, and took her hand. "I'm sorry, I don't know what to say, dear."

Debra stood, shaking while she wiped her handkerchief across her eyes. She turned toward the mayor. "I'm sorry, Mister Miller. My Daddy made me promise not to say anything to anyone about this. And … I promised." Debra eased down into her chair and held her mother's hand.

For a full minute on the calm spring day, an easy breeze crept through an open window of the courtroom. The breeze worked alone. No sound came from anywhere in the room.

Mayor Miller eased up from his chair and looked around at the crowd. With a light rap of the gavel and a calm voice, he announced, "This court is in recess until further notice."

Chapter Sixteen

Hardy opened the door to his room. He wore a big smile, yet tears filled his eyes. The four days he'd been locked up seemed like months. Even one night in a chicken coop would make any man appreciate home.

He checked his clock on the shelf. The café would be closed now. Maybe he could get a decent meal tomorrow. At least he would have a real bed to sleep in. His room may not be the cleanest he'd ever lived in, but it definitely smelled better than a chicken coop.

He crashed onto the bed and closed his eyes. A minute later, a knock on the door brought him to his feet. On his way to the door, he wondered if he should open it. He'd had a lot of trouble in the last few days. The person who knocked may be wanting to cause more.

The knock sounded once more, and someone yelled, "Hardy, you in there?" He tripped the latch and opened the door to two of the most welcome faces he'd seen in a while. His heart grew excited.

"Wayne and Wanda. Oh, my God. It's so great to see both of you."

Hardy found seats for all of them and tried to answer their endless questions. He told them the whole story, not sure they believed the part about the Watts brothers.

"One thing we do know," Wanda told him. "You are the best employee we ever had. The days you missed seemed very long to the two of us also. We hope it's all over for your sake and ours. So, tell us you'll be at work tomorrow morning, and we will sleep good tonight."

Hardy nodded. "If nobody comes here and hauls me off to the lockup again, I'll be at work in the morning. I need to earn some more money." He pulled his door key from his pocket. "This is all they left me."

Before the Walkers left, they gave him two quarters. "This is the least we can do, "Wayne told him. "If you can prove what you told us, Luther Watts should be locked up for stealing your money."

At the café the next morning, Hardy wolfed down his breakfast and bought another breakfast biscuit to take with him. He did not know what to expect from the people who pressed charges against him. Mayor Miller released Hardy, telling him his fate may depend on what the Watts family would do in the days ahead.

Hardy had tried to tell the mayor the whole story, but the mayor would not permit it. "I can't put myself in an awkward position like that," Max told him. "I want to know, and I hope I do when this thing is over."

Two days after, the lockup guards came to the store and rearrested Hardy.

Convinced he could take both of them, Hardy wanted to fight them off. Instead, he fought off the temptation, knowing a fight … win, lose, or draw … would be stupid. The guards locked him in the chicken coop once more.

The next day, Hardy's hope and confidence rose to a new level when the Walkers eagerly sat in the courtroom, addressed the jury and the people of the community, and told them that what they believed all along is the truth, that Hardy Brooke is a decent, stand-up guy.

Hardy sat up straight and breathed deep, his chest expanding, until the mayor granted Luther Watts the opportunity to question the witnesses. Hardy's hopes took a nosedive.

Like before, Luther strutted up front. "Mister Hardy, for the benefit of all those watching, would you stand, please?"

Hardy stood. His muscles tightened. His busted lip, though now nearly healed, convinced him it was his turn to fatten a lip on Luther's face. Hardy clenched his fist while his arm shook. He looked at the Walkers seated near him. Wayne's expression said *no*. Wanda's expression pleaded, *don't you dare do that here*.

Wearing a big smile, Luther turned to the Walkers. "Great to see you two again. That was an inspiring speech. It's nice to know your friend has so many good qualities."

His lips tightened as he nodded. "However, we didn't hear anything negative. I'm sure we'll all agree that nobody is perfect. That means you must have left out something." He jerked his head toward Hardy but kept his eyes on Wayne Walker. "How long has this man worked for you?"

"About a year," Mrs. Walker replied.

"Are you telling us, Mister and Mrs. Walker, that Hardy Brooke has done nothing you thought was wrong or that disappointed you? Is that possible?"

Wanda cleared her throat. "We had to teach him about how we do things in the store. But he learned fast, so I can't say I was disappointed."

Luther turned to Wayne. "Okay, does he have any duties outside the store?"

Wayne wrinkled his nose. "He wasn't thrilled about moving the outhouse. But he did it."

Chuckles filled the room, including those from Mayor Miller and the jury.

Luther did not chuckle nor smile but leaned toward Wayne.

We know you sell tools, firewood, and small quantities of lumber. You have a mule and a wagon to deliver things or to bring merchandise to your store. Does Mister Brooke deal with any of that?"

"He does," Wayne said.

Wanda's face paled.

"So … neither of you have ever been disappointed by anything Mister Brooke has done inside or *outside* your store?"

No one in the courtroom made a sound while Luther waited. After a long minute, he turned and addressed the jury. "Well, ladies and gentlemen, if these two refuse to answer the question, I think we can assume the answer."

Wayne raised his hand. "Not long after Hardy came to work for us, he had a slight accident with the wagon. We repaired it, and everything is good."

Luther turned to Wanda. "Mrs. Walker, would you help your husband? Tell us a bit more about that accident, please. We'd like to hear what caused the damage to the wagon."

Wanda pulled a handkerchief from her pocket and wiped her face. "I didn't deal with that situation. My husband could answer that much better."

Luther bent toward her. "Just tell us what you know about it, please. That's all I'm asking."

"Hardy went to pick up a load of firewood for us, and on the way, he ran into a lot of wind and rain. The mule panicked and took off in a wild run. Hardy jumped out of the wagon to save his own life, and the wagon hit the edge of the door frame when the mule pulled the wagon into a barn. Wayne and Hardy repaired the wagon the next day, and it's still in good shape." She grinned. "And Melvin, our mule, is still in good shape."

112

People in the courtroom laughed. When the room grew quiet, he leaned toward Wanda and stuck his face close to hers. "So, the mule pulled the wagon into a barn. Tell us please, Mrs. Walker … where is that barn?"

She turned to her husband, her face showing a plea for help.

Wayne's face lost color. "That barn? It's, well, it's not here in town. So, it doesn't really matter."

"Okay, if it doesn't matter, tell us where it is, and we'll let the jury decide."

By the time Luther finished probing, the Walkers had revealed the whole story about when Hardy tried to escape to his former world.

Hardy drew a long, deep breath and let it go. *I sure hope Seth can rescue me.*

***

When the trial broke for lunch, Hardy wanted to cry on his way to the lockup. But he knew most who saw him would consider that a sign of weakness, and he refused to be weak. He held up his head while the guards unlocked the door.

To Hardy's surprise, Mayor Miller showed up right behind him and dismissed the guards. "You two can go for lunch. I need to visit with this man for a few minutes." Wearing smiles, the men left the key with the mayor, turned, and hurried away. Miller untied Hardy's hands.

"Hardy, if you don't have money for lunch today, I'll buy."

"Thank you, sir. The Walkers gave me some money, so I can buy lunch for *you* today."

"Thanks, but we can't do it that way. I just wanted to tell you something you already know. Your character witnesses, no matter how much they wanted to help, didn't help at all."

Hardy nodded. "Yeah, I guess that was obvious. I'm hoping Seth's testimony will make up for what happened this morning. But in case it doesn't, I would like to have a pencil and a few sheets of paper."

"I can get them for you. May I ask the reason?"

"Yes, sir. I want to write down the full story of what happened at the creek that day and the following morning. I want to give it to you, so you will know exactly what happened. If you don't want to read it right away, I understand. Or, if you want to share it with the jury, that would be okay, too."

"I like your idea, Hardy. Hand it to me when you're done, and I'll decide the best time to read it and who to share it with. Now, what would you like for lunch? I'm buying."

Hardy's face lit up. "A big ham sandwich and some fried potatoes."

"I'll see you as soon as I can get it." The mayor left without locking the door and returned in ten minutes with Hardy's order and one of the same for himself. After lunch, he gave Hardy the pencil and sheets of paper he asked for.

"The café owner gave these to me as soon as I told him why I needed them. I'm convinced he's on your side. I'm also convinced most of the people in this town are with you on this, but I have no feel for the jury's impression so far."

He looked down and up again. "And I wouldn't tell you if I knew."

Chapter Seventeen

Suspense plagued Hardy while he waited for Seth's afternoon testimony. The man seemed confident and relaxed, and he was a good speaker. Seth had missed the morning session and could not know how underhanded and driven Luther could be.

After Seth told the jury how he arranged Hardy's move from *his* world to this one, Luther strutted up the aisle.

"Seth, great to see you again." He stopped in front of the witness. "I admire and appreciate your work. You bring some great people to our small town and likely have a tough job selecting the right people for this lifestyle."

He looked around. "Now, ladies and gentlemen, I have never been to any town other than ours. But we know the kind of people we want to live here. In spite of Mister Seth's golden record, we all make mistakes."

Luther swallowed a long drink from the corner water bucket and threw the dipper into place, splashing water all over the table. He wiped his mouth on his sleeve while he strutted toward Seth.

"So, tell us, kind sir, have you ever made a mistake in your job?"

Seth gave him a slow nod. "Of course, don't you make mistakes in *your* job?"

Luther stood tall and straight. "That's my point. We all make mistakes. But I'm happy to hear that you recognize your own. So, tell us, please, all the mistakes you made in bringing Hardy Brooke into our world and why he obviously does not belong here."

Seth grinned and shook his head. "You might have it all upside down. Maybe you're the one who does not belong here."

Mouths hung open in the courtroom while wide-eyed observers scanned the crowd as if looking for permission to laugh.

Luther stared at the floor and then looked up at the mayor. "Sir, would you please tell this witness to answer my questions?"

The mayor stood. "Gentlemen, this is to *both* of you. Don't turn this testimony into an argument. Mister Luther, if you will dispense with the insults directed at the witness, I believe he will answer more of your questions."

The mayor moved a step closer and looked at Seth. "Please focus on questions and answers, not on accusations and insults from both sides. Thank you."

Luther plunged ahead as if determined to trip up his witness. He asked Seth how he met Hardy and why he thought Hardy was a good candidate.

Seth told him about the hospital where Hardy suffered from an injury and needed help.

"After I learned about his grandparents dying in a tragic accident, and then both of his parents were killed in a crash, I knew he had a heavy load to deal with. I thought then, and I think now, that he *was* and *is* a great candidate. He is an upstanding young man in our town, works hard, makes friends easily, the kind we need here."

Luther appeared to struggle with every reply from Seth. At one point, he threw up his hands. "So, tell us, Mister perfect ambassador, why was Mister Brooke in the hospital? Did he suffer from a mental problem? Did he do something to cause his own injury?"

Seth sat up straight. "Hardy suffered from a hip injury. He could barely walk, and my heart went out to him. That's how the conversations started. As we talked, I learned more about him and believed he was a good candidate."

Seth pulled a handkerchief from his pocket and wiped his brow, wondering why Luther struggled to find something unfavorable about Hardy.

Luther probed about Hardy's injury. When Seth finally had to tell him that a gun caused the hip injury, Luther went crazy with accusations and exaggerations about Hardy's previous life.

When the charade finally ended, Hardy looked around through the crowd, reading people's faces. Luther caused a lot of damage.

Hardy's breath grew ragged as he wiped his eyes on his sleeve. At the end of the two testimonies, the jurors' faces told him he was now in deeper trouble.

Mayor Miller stood and addressed the crowd. "Ladies and gentlemen, we have seen this hearing, and now this *trial*, drag on far too long, with little, if any, hard evidence. Neither side has proved its case. However, our law considers a defendant innocent until proven guilty. So, I am going to dismiss the jury and put this trial on hold until the party making the claim can produce an eyewitness or hard evidence against the defendant, Mister Hardy Brooke."

Jody Watts jumped to his feet. "Mayor Miller, I have the eyewitness sitting right here beside me. She will testify tomorrow with the full story of what happened during the twenty-four hours she was missing from our home. Her testimony will be the solid evidence we need against Mister Brooke."

People shuffled in their seats. A buzz of low talk and loud whispers scattered through the crowd.

Mayor Miller rapped the gavel. "Ladies and gentlemen, your attention, please." The crowd ignored him. He rapped the gavel once more and spoke louder. "Ladies and gentlemen, if you want to remain in this courtroom for the next three minutes and if you want my permission to attend tomorrow, I need your attention *now*."

A sudden silence fell in the room while the mayor glared. He nodded at Debra.

"Debra Watts, would you stand, please?" When she stood, the mayor sat in his chair and grabbed his notepad.

"Debra, please don't take what I am about to say as criticism. I do not mean it that way. But the last two times you spoke to us here, you had little to offer. I can understand that you were very uneasy, talking about something private that must have made you uncomfortable. Before we schedule your testimony, can you tell us if you feel comfortable enough to do that this time?" Will you stand here tomorrow morning and give us a complete explanation of what happened on the day you encountered Mister Hardy Brooke by the creek?"

She wiped her tears with her hand. "Yes, sir. I will tell you everything. I promise." Debra covered her face and cried.

***

The following morning, the local news reporter scribbled words as fast as he could write while the overflow crowd at the town café talked about nothing but the trial. He had covered the action and inaction in the courtroom for a few days and found little news worth reporting.

Twice, he approached the Watts family and asked for interviews. Jody Watts would not permit anyone in the family to talk to a newspaper reporter. But here today, many speculated on the outcome, and the ace reporter found much to write about.

***

118

Before 8:30, the crowd gathered in front of the courthouse doors. The reporter gathered with them. Some talked aloud. Most mumbled and whispered. Some claimed to be fans of the defendant, while others believed the jury would convict Hardy Brooke. Everyone hoped Debra Watts would tell the whole story as she had promised.

At 9:30, as if someone tripped a switch, the noisy crowd in the courtroom fell into sudden silence except those who scrambled to their seats. For nearly half an hour, Mayor Miller waited for the star witness to appear. The over-eager crowd had seen not one member of the Watts family today.

Mayor Miller stood and held up his open hand. "Ladies and gentlemen, our key witness has not yet shown up today. But we will proceed."

He asked a guard to untie Hardy's hands. With the tie string gone, Hardy got up and rubbed his wrists. Mayor Miller turned toward Hardy, had him say his name, and then directed him to "Raise your right hand and repeat after me."

After the oath, the mayor said, "Mister Hardy Brooke, in your own words, please tell this jury how and where you met Debra Watts and what happened afterward."

Hardy cleared his throat. "Ladies and gentlemen, a few days ago, I had no idea that I would be in a courtroom explaining a single day in my life. But I am here, and I will tell you the truth."

Hardy told the jurors about crossing the bridge over the creek and how it made him want to explore. He told them about the cries for help, how he ran alongside the creek searching for the person in trouble, and about his bloody nose before he found that person. He told them of the short conversations he had with Debra, how she wound up sleeping behind him, still there when the Watts brothers found them the next morning.

While Hardy told the jurors everything, he watched the expressions on their faces and told himself they believed him.

A guard summoned Mayor Miller to a small room. Within five minutes the long-faced Mayor slouched toward his desk. Mouths hung open while he rapped the gavel.

"Ladies and gentlemen, I am sorry to report this to you. I know you have been waiting patiently for this trial to end. But this trial is less important than the safety of a child. I had a conversation with Mrs. Watts in the office. She tells me that Debra, her daughter, is missing. Debra's father and uncle are out searching for her."

The mayor delivered a hard rap with the gavel. "Everyone stand, please, and let's say a one-minute silent prayer for Debra and the family."

Hardy said a silent prayer along with the crowd but breathed a huge sigh of relief. After the courtroom closed, he pleaded with Mayor Miller to let him sleep in his own room, in a real bed.

"You know, Mayor Miller, I will be here tomorrow morning and in the courtroom before 9 o'clock."

The mayor nodded. "I know, Hardy. But I have concerns for your safety. I'll have a guard outside the door all night. If anything goes wrong between now and then, some people in this town will be ready to string you up." The mayor chuckled. "So, you'll have to stay in that lovely chicken coop for one more night."

With eyes closed, Hardy raised his head. *Thank you, God, for watching over Debra and for Mayor Miller's wisdom.*

Back in the lockup, Hardy ordered a chicken dinner and coffee for lunch. *What the heck. If I have to live like a chicken, may as well eat a chicken.*

Hardy expected the guard who took his order would deliver it. He felt glad to be wrong. Mayor Miller brought two chicken dinners, one for Hardy and one for himself.

"I brought this to you because I have some news to share. I hope you'll agree it's *good* news."

Hardy pointed to his chicken-stuffed jaw, trying to say, *I can't talk right now.*

The mayor nodded. "Just thought you'd like to know Mrs. Watts returned minutes ago. The two men found Debra."

The mayor swallowed his first bite, then continued.

"Debra's mom said she and the girl are fine physically, but she's concerned about her daughter's mind. Debra is having problems deciding what to do most of the time and often appears depressed."

Hardy downed a big gulp of coffee. "Well, Max, I'm not a psychologist, but Debra's father is her biggest problem. He wants her to tell the jury I mistreated her. She doesn't want to say that. She knows I saved her life, and none of that other stuff is true. But Jody believes all the bad stuff and wants me punished. So, along with help from Luther, Jody Watts has to convince his daughter to lie to the jury."

Hardy rubbed the lump in his throat. "And she might do that because she's tired of being intimidated by her father and uncle. And…she gets no support from her mother."

Hardy's eyes grew misty. "If that happens, her life will be ruined right along with mine. She will never forgive her father or her uncle. But worst of all, she will never forgive *herself.*"

He wiped his eyes. "That poor child is only eleven years old. She's no match for two grown men, both authority figures who try to badger her into saying what *they* think is true."

"Honestly, Hardy, I didn't know you were that smart, but I believe you are exactly right. What you just said is what I wanted to hear from you, except in the courtroom before the jury. I don't want the stuff you say here to interfere with my judgment of this case."

Hardy sighed. "I'm not under oath, but I couldn't improve my case by lying to you. Besides, I wrote down everything and gave you the paper this morning at the courthouse."

Miller nodded. "It's in my desk. We'll see what happens tomorrow."

Hardy swallowed his last bite of chicken, downed another gulp of coffee, and wiped his mouth on his sleeve. "Do you know where the Watts brothers found Debra?"

The Mayor grinned. "I do. What are you thinking?"

Hardy looked into the man's eyes. "I'm betting it was the same place by the creek."

"You won your bet."

"I'd also bet that Jody and Luther hoped they would find me there with her so they could kill me and get away with it."

"Think about this, Mayor Miller. If Debra had been abused in that location, would she ever return there of her own free will? Luther may never allow himself to realize that or care. But I think Debra's father *would*."

Chapter Eighteen

For many years, *The Mystique Weekly* published a Saturday newspaper to keep Mystique's residents up to date on critical news. This week, a rare Thursday afternoon edition appeared, headlined *Debra Watts Disappears Again*.

The story told how Debra's father and uncle found her a few hours later by Mystique Creek, in the same location as before.

A short interview with Mayor Miller assured residents the trial was set to reconvene at 9:00 A.M. Friday.

The topic became an instant buzz among the lunch crowd at the café, barbershop, grocery market, along with many customers at the General Store. Someone suggested the blacksmith may be the only one who had not heard the story by Friday morning, when the largest crowd ever gathered in front of the courthouse.

At 8:30 AM, Mayor Miller stepped out the front door of the courthouse and waved at the crowd but got no one's attention. He called out to them many times, but they would not be distracted from the chaos.

Mayor Miller squeezed through the door again, grabbed the bullhorn and a chair, and carried them outside. He stood on the chair and, with help from a security guard, got the crowd's attention."

The guard weaved his way through the people, shouting, "Quiet, please. The mayor needs to talk to you." A minute after, nothing but whispers floated through the crowd with all eyes fixed on the mayor. He set the bullhorn aside and raised his voice.

"Good morning, everyone. I'm guessing all of you here would like to attend the trial this morning. However, as we predicted, we cannot accommodate everyone. We have room for sixty-two people. In a couple of minutes, we will draw numbers to determine who gets in. If you draw a number sixty-two or less, you will be admitted. Sorry, that's all the room we have."

Mayor Miller tipped his hat. "Thank you for your patience. See you inside. Please keep it orderly."

At 9 o'clock, the mayor rapped his gavel. "This court is now in session. Be seated, please. And please show your respect and keep the room quiet.

From his usual chair, Hardy scanned the crowd. Although, at this point in the trial, only one person in the room mattered. She sat in the chair between her parents without moving or looking around. Her pale face and lack of motion told him she was afraid. How could she *not* be?

Fear tore through Hardy's gut. *That eleven-year-old child holds my entire future in her hands or, at least, in her words.*

Rattling paper turned Hardy's attention toward Mayor Miller when the man opened a desk drawer and pulled out a folded yellow paper. He spread it flat on his desk and laid a pencil on top of it.

The mayor made a short speech about how the trial had proceeded from the start. "We are at the final phase, and hoping the witness here today will share with us … the truth, the whole truth, and nothing but the truth." He asked Debra to stand.

"Debra Watts, we believe you know your testimony here today is the most important part of this trial. Are you ready to give us the true and complete story exactly the way it happened?"

She nodded.

"Very good. Would you answer aloud for us, please?"

"I will do what you asked me to do, sir."

Debra's father hugged her and patted her back. She walked down the aisle toward the stage while surprised people stared.

Jody Watts jumped from his chair. "Debra, you can testify while you're sitting right here beside us."

Debra stopped but did not turn around.

Mayor Miller rapped the gavel once more, and yelled, "Sit down and keep your silence, Mister Watts. Or I will have you removed from this courtroom until this trial is finished."

Debra continued, stopping at the steps that led up to the stage. She turned, folded her hands, and looked at Mayor Miller. "Is it time for me to start?"

Light giggles spread throughout the room while the mayor smiled and nodded. "Yes, dear, you can come up on the stage so people can hear you better."

She walked up the steps, took a deep breath, then turned and folded her shaking hands.

"I don't know how to do this." She paused. "So, I'll just tell you what happened."

"I, uhm, woke up early that Sunday morning, and I wanted to go for a walk by myself. That's what I thought I was supposed to do when I grew up. And I thought I would grow up faster if I started right away. So, I sneaked my brother's new blue jeans out of the closet and put them on. They made me feel stronger like I could do anything I wanted. I got his hat and put it on with my hair stuffed up under it."

"Then I went out into the woods to take a walk. I went out there before with my parents and brother and once with a friend, but she's older than me."

"This time, I felt a lot more grown-up than I ever had. I saw stuff I never noticed before like a frog scratching the side of his head. I kept walking, looking at all the birds and the squirrels, and I saw two turtles."

Debra pulled a tissue from her pocket and wiped her face. "Pretty soon, I knew I had to get home to eat breakfast and get ready for church. But then, I didn't know which way to go. So, I walked a little bit one way and then the other way, but I didn't know which one was right. I could hear some water splashing somewhere, and I was so thirsty that I went over there to get a drink."

Debra told about climbing a tree to help find her way out, and how she fell into the creek and hurt her arm.

She wiped a tear and rubbed her left shoulder. "It hurt really bad, and I couldn't hang onto anything with it, so I had to use my right hand to hang on to that big root thing."

"I kept crying and screaming, and I was more scared than ever in my life. After a really long time, I heard somebody behind me, and I let go of the root thing because I thought it was my daddy. But it was Hardy, and he helped me up on his back and carried me to the bank."

Debra told the spellbound people in front of her about all the things Hardy did to help her. "He thought I was a boy when he saw me in the hat and blue jeans. So, when we got to the bank, he said I should take off my shirt and hang it on a limb to dry faster. I said *no*. Then I told him my name, and he said he was sorry for thinking I was a boy."

She told how Hardy piled leaves by the tree to help keep her warm, about the hoot owl that scared her, and how she ran over to Hardy's tree and snuggled up behind him.

While Debra spoke, Mayor Miller followed her story on the papers from Hardy and often made check marks on the page.

The courtroom sat in dead silence while everyone stared. Debra came down the steps, turned, and walked toward Hardy. He stood, and she grabbed his waist and hugged him.

"Mister Hardy, you saved my life, and I will never forget you." She backed up and looked at him. "Please don't let them lock you up or be mean to you. You didn't do anything wrong. Can we still be friends, please?"

She grabbed his tied hands, turned, and looked at her father.

"I'm sorry, Daddy, but I had to tell everybody here what really happened. And I have to tell them Hardy is a real good friend. If he didn't come along, I would've drowned."

She looked out at the crowd. "Please don't do anything to hurt Mister Hardy. No matter what anybody tells you. He didn't do anything wrong."

Mayor Miller stood, thanked Debra, and turned to Hardy. "Mister Brooke, after hearing your testimony yesterday and Debra's today, I believe it's time to turn this case over to the jury. Do you have anything to add before I proceed?

"Thank you, Mayor, but there's nothing to add. Debra made sure of that."

Jody and Luther Watts stood and stared at Debra, their puzzled, wide-eyed faces telling everyone what they felt.

People in the audience stood, shaking their heads, and smiling. Someone applauded, and then everyone applauded.

Debra's mother clapped and cried as she walked toward her daughter. She stopped and gave her a big hug. "I love you, Debra. Thank you for telling everything."

Mayor Miller stood, held up his hand, and asked for silence. "Ladies and gentlemen, I think we can now send this case to the jury. Would the jury proceed to the meeting room to discuss your decision?"

The jury foreman got up and smiled. "Mayor Miller, and everyone here in the courtroom, I believe the jury has already reached a verdict." He looked at the other jurors as each one nodded then turned to Mayor Miller.

"We, the jury, find the defendant *not guilty*."

Mayor Miller picked up his bullhorn and shouted above the applause and cheers. "Thank you all. The verdict is in. This trial is closed. You are all dismissed."

Pocket knife in hand, he walked toward the victor. "Congratulations, Hardy." He opened his knife and cut the rope that bound Hardy's wrists. "You're a free man. Justice has prevailed."

* * *

Hardy finished his steak dinner, feeling grateful yet still amazed, while he looked up from his table in the café. Dozens of people from the courtroom crowd, local business owners, and townspeople he'd never met stopped by, shook his hand, and congratulated him.

He learned how the Walkers, along with Seth, Sam, the blacksmith, Jeff, the chef, and Nelda Miller, planned this event starting almost a week ago. They all believed in Hardy's total innocence. They also believed the jury would acquit, and they came to celebrate.

Hardy learned the organizers kept their plan a tight secret. Nelda worked hard to keep her husband, along with members of the jury, the Watts family, and the news reporter, from learning about the celebration. But they invited everyone as soon as the trial ended.

Hardy appreciated all who came but found some difficult to deal with. Most conversations were awkward, and he could think of nothing to say when the Watts family stopped by his table. He stood, nodded, and offered a slight smile.

Debra hugged him and thanked him again. Mrs. Watts did not hug him but thanked him twice for rescuing her daughter. Jody Watts did not hug or thank him but congratulated him on his victory and offered a halfhearted apology.

Hardy pointed toward Debra. "She's the one who deserves the credit. I couldn't have done it without her."

Debra blushed but did not speak.

His biggest surprise came after most of the guests left. Only Seth and the Walkers remained at Hardy's table when Luther Watts showed his face. Hardy stood and stared as the man approached. He would not shake hands with Luther nor accept an apology. He would not forgive that dirty lowlife for his underhanded tactics while he tried to get him convicted. But Luther Watts did not offer his hand nor an apology. He stopped a few feet in front of Hardy and offered congratulations. To Hardy, it sounded like a sneer.

The man dug two quarters from his pocket and held them in Hardy's face. "A couple of people said I owe you these. So here they are. Now we're even."

Hardy squeezed his right fist around the coins, held them up, and glanced around the room. Debra's parents waited near the front door. She stood near them and they watched Hardy as if waiting for something to happen.

Hardy was so proud of her. She showed courage to do the right thing, to tell the truth despite her father's wishes and her uncle's insistence. Hardy needed to square things, but now would be the wrong time.

"You paid *one* debt, Luther. But we're not even. Someday, with your hands tied behind you, I'm gonna bust you in the face like a boulder smashing a rotten grape. You can count on it, weasel."

Hardy turned and waved goodbye to his three friends still at the table. "Thanks for the party. I'll never forget it." When he looked back, Luther Watts had gone.

Chapter Nineteen

Hardy opened the door to his room, stepped inside, and drew a long, deep breath. He looked at the clock on the shelf. "Of course," he said aloud, "the clock ran down. Gotta rewind it and reset it."

He picked up the small mirror next to the clock, looked at his face, and smiled. The nightmare was over—no more time in the chicken coop jail. No depending on other people to get a meal. No more spending a night on a filthy, smelly cot and hoping for sleep.

His busted lip had healed, probably faster than Luther Watts' busted pride would. He glanced in the mirror and nodded at himself. "Life is good."

Thoughts of the last few days ran through his mind as he prepared for bed. He would replace those thoughts and focus on something positive and pleasant that happened tonight, something that would not likely leave his mind for a long while.

Before he finished his meal at the café, Nelda Miller had brought a young lady to his table.

"Hardy, this is Maria. She lives with Max and me, and I don't think you two have met."

Hardy's mouth fell open. "No. We have not." He turned to Nelda. "How did you keep this beautiful young lady a secret? How long has she been living with you?"

A big smile crossed Maria's pink face as Nelda replied. "About six months. She doesn't get out much, but she came with Max and me tonight so she could meet new people."

Hardy sat up straight. "Thank you, Nelda. I'm glad to be one of those people." He tapped his mouth while he stared at Maria. "Sorry, I didn't mean to be too bold, but I don't often meet a young lady like you."

He turned to Nelda. "Is she your daughter, niece, cousin, or a real princess?"

Nelda smiled. "She's our housekeeper, but she's like a daughter to us. We have no children of our own, and we kind-of adopted her. That's why her last name is now *Miller*, same as ours. And she's a delight to have around."

Hardy looked at her and nodded. "Yeah, I'll bet she is."

He grinned. "You're with a great family. You haven't been to the café very often. Otherwise, I would've talked to you." Hardy felt the heat on his face. "Sorry, Maria. I don't want to embarrass you. It's just that I…"

Maria shrugged. "It's okay, Hardy." After a shy smile, she angled her head at Mrs. Miller. "Like Nelda said, I don't get out much. But I'd like to meet you here again so we can talk."

"I'd like that, too. I work at the General Store. Next time you come in, find me and say hello."

She leaned toward him and with a slight smile, said, "I will."

From the corner of his eye, Hardy saw Wanda Walker. He turned to see her bright eyes and big grin. He would hear about this tomorrow. *But that would be quite all right.*

***

The next morning, Hardy felt grateful and delighted to be at work, and the Walkers were happy to have him. He worked harder than ever, trying to show them he appreciated all they did for him.

132

But Wanda surprised him. She waited until after lunch to ask about Maria.

"Hardy, you seemed quite taken with that young lady last night." She giggled. "I know it's none of my business, but did you really like her? Or … were you just being nice?"

Hardy chuckled. "Oh, I'm shocked you would ask."

Wayne laughed out loud. "Oh, me too. I can't believe she would want to know."

Hardy grinned. "Well if you must know … *both*. I was trying to be nice, and I'm also very interested." He looked at Wayne and rolled his eyes.

Hardy turned to Wanda. "I want to get to know her, but I don't know what to do. I would like a date. But, here in Mystique, I have no idea where to take her or how to get there."

After a long drink from the water bucket, he turned to Wanda. "Got any ideas?"

"Yes, I do. Get in touch with her and meet her at the café. Just the two of you at the table, no one else. Have a meal and get acquainted. Treat her nice. Women love that. After the two of you talk for a few minutes…remember to let her talk also … you will think of where to go and what to do for your next date. It really is that simple. Trust me."

Hardy trusted. A week after their chat at the café, he suggested giving her a ride in the buckboard, so she could explore much more of the area. She agreed.

When Hardy asked the Walkers if he could borrow the buckboard and the mule to take Maria for a ride, Wayne agreed.

"Hardy, you *can't* be serious," Wanda said. "You call a ride in a buckboard a *date*? After she bounces around on a wooden seat for a half-hour, you may never get another date. And I wouldn't blame her."

Hardy's face grew pale. "It's not like I have a golden chariot. We need some time together, with nobody else around."

Wayne broke in. "Yeah, Wanda. You said they need some time alone. Remember?"

"Hah." Wanda wrinkled her face. "Not in a big ugly buckboard." She gripped Hardy's collar. "Show a little romance, Hardy. You're not taking her out to pick up a load of firewood or supplies. Use our horse and buggy."

Wayne laughed. "I can't argue with that, Hardy. You know, there are certain things women understand so much better than men. Most of the time, we do what works without thinking about the other angle."

Hardy's face reddened as he giggled. "I, uhm, would've never asked to borrow your horse and buggy, but I'll certainly take you up on that."

On the following Sunday afternoon, Hardy sat up straight and proud as he drove the buggy to Miller's Place. After brief greetings with Max and Nelda, Hardy helped Maria into the buggy. He drove toward the road, trying hard to appear casual instead of proud. He failed.

Maxwell Miller's field hands, Barney, and Cecil, watched everything. Hardy would not turn and look at them but pictured them standing there paralyzed by envy, with their tongues hanging out. On the outside, Hardy smiled. On the inside, he screamed with delight.

At the road, he went left. He'd wanted to explore Never Ending Road since he rode Handsome Devil here more than a year ago. Now, it would be much better than he had dreamed. Hardy had Princess Maria by his side.

***

While the horse pulled the buggy, Hardy and Maria watched a variety of wildlife on the ground, frogs and fish in a pond, crows, cardinals, and a falcon in the air beneath silver-blue skies. The two walked and talked, held hands, and laughed. They shared likes and dislikes, funny stories, dreams, and wishes.

They lingered at a white birch tree and carved their initials in the bark with Hardy's pocketknife. Maria leaned against the tree and gazed into his eyes. He gazed into hers and kissed her.

Hardy knew their date ended too soon when he kissed her the second and third time on the front porch of her home while the sun sank low on the horizon. He whispered, "I'd love to see you every day. I mean, …very soon."

She smiled and whispered "Me, too," and went inside.

In the middle of the night, Hardy snapped awake often. *His date with Maria? Did it actually happen? Or was it merely a fantasy? It must be real. It's much too good to be a dream.*

He dozed off many times during the night, his mind replaying everything from the start.

Now, he lay awake, delighted, while it all played over and over in his mind until a slight interference crept in. *You can't fall in love on a first date, Hardy.*

Monday morning, the clock alarmed far too early. Hardy stumbled out of bed, knowing the alarm clock must be wrong. He grabbed his pocket watch, a gift from the Walkers when the trial ended. *An obvious conspiracy,* he told himself. The alarm clock and pocket watch agreed.

He washed his face in the cool water of the wash pan, then dabbed his fingers in the water and raked them through his hair to help him wake up.

He grabbed his coffee mug from the cupboard and headed to the café, rubbing his face again while he walked. He always enjoyed familiar faces in the dining room. *But today, I don't want to see anyone I know. I feel and look so rough this morning.*

The bells on the door jingled as Hardy walked in, and, like always, most people looked up to see who came in or left.

Max Miller sat on the backside of the table near the far wall and looked up at Hardy. Across from Max, with her back toward Hardy, sat a beautiful, red-haired young lady. Hardy's eyes saw only the back of her head. His memory saw that beautiful face and those kissable lips. Max waved and motioned for Hardy to join them.

On his uneasy walk toward them, Hardy knew he could share a table and conversation with either Max or Maria. But both at once? That could get awkward from the start. He approached Max's side of the table.

"Good morning, Mister Miller." He looked across the table and stared without thinking. "Good morning to you too, Princess."

She blushed. "Good morning, Hardy. Hope you slept well."

"Oh yes. I had a great night, and hope you did."

Max scratched his chin while he looked at her and then at Hardy. "I don't usually ask questions like this, and I'm not asking now. But … as you two left yesterday afternoon, Nelda and I believe it's a natural fit for both of you." Max sipped his coffee while he glanced from one to the other.

Getting no response, he smiled and continued. "This morning, Nelda told me you two talked yesterday afternoon and got better acquainted."

With big eyes and a pink face, Maria drew back.

136

Max continued. "I was happy to hear that. She's a fine young lady." He looked at Hardy. "And you're a fine young man."

When Hardy's usual breakfast sandwich arrived, he told Max and Maria he had to get an early start for work. He took his sandwich and coffee with him.

After breakfast in his room, Hardy stepped downstairs to go to work, knowing Wanda would ask questions this morning about him and Maria and want to know if they had planned another date.

Chapter Twenty

While he cleaned and restocked the high shelves in the store, Hardy heard footsteps. They stopped behind him. He turned and looked down at a beautiful, smiling face.

"Maria, I wasn't expecting you, but what a treat. You need help with something?"

"Yes, I do." She pulled a cloth cover from the wicker basket she carried. "I brought some food, and if you didn't have lunch yet, I'm hoping you will help me eat this."

Hardy laughed. "Seems the *least* I could do since you came all this way."

In the covered area for firewood, the couple found a private spot to enjoy lunch.

Before they began, Hardy pulled her close. "I'd like to tell you this is an old custom, but the truth is, it's a *new* custom I want to start. We should always do this before a meal." He gave her a big kiss.

With a huge grin, she said, "New, old, or neither. I like it."

They talked and laughed and teased each other while they ate. Hardy looked at everything she brought. "You must've worked hard to put all this together. I guess Nelda approved?"

"Approved? This was her idea. She made this lunch for us and convinced me to bring it to you.". I know you're going to say...*are you kidding me*? So, I'll tell you right off. I'm not kidding. She likes you, Hardy. A lot"

Hardy nodded. "She told me that on the night you and I met, sitting at the table in the café. I wasn't surprised she likes me, but surprised she *said* it."

"Well, it's true. She doesn't say that about everybody because, truthfully, she doesn't like *everybody*."

"I think *everybody* knows that. But I'm curious. Did she offer anything more than today's lunch, like suggestions concerning you and me?"

"She did. She asked me if you had mentioned another date. I didn't know what to say, except *we're working on it*. So, she offered an idea."

Hardy focused on Maria's eyes. "Wanna tell me?"

"You likely know Max and Nelda have two great riding horses, and Nelda said we could take them out for a ride if you want."

Hardy laughed. "It's as if she read my mind. But do you like to ride? If so, I'll—"

"I love to ride. Never had my own horse, but I've been riding with friends since I was seven, and I'm not a bad rider."

"Well, what do you say we go for a ride on Sunday afternoon?"

"I'd love it. After church, you come to our house for dinner, and we'll go for a ride afterward?"

Hardy shrugged. "I couldn't dream of a better plan. But...don't you have to square it with Nelda about Sunday dinner?"

With a big grin, Maria said, "I already did."

At the sound of shuffling feet, Hardy and Maria looked up. Wayne walked toward them, pocket watch in hand.

Hardy stood and whispered, "I forgot about the time. Gotta get to work." After a quick kiss, he said hello to Wayne while Maria gathered up the basket.

***

On Sunday afternoon, Hardy left Melvin in Max Miller's barn. An hour after a great meal, Hardy and Maria saddled two impressive horses. Max and Nelda gave them pointers on the personality of each horse.

As they mounted the horses, Hardy tried once again to conceal his pride while Barney and Cecil appeared ready to slobber as they watched Maria swing into the saddle.

Hardy pretended not to notice. But his thoughts were saying, *eat your heart out*, as he and his girlfriend rode off.

Hardy sat up straight, his face a big smile, as they turned left once again onto the road. "I've wanted to do this for more than a year, ride a horse down Never-Ending Road."

Maria laughed. "I know. You mentioned it before. But why do you find it so fascinating?"

"On my first day in this town, Seth called this Never-Ending Road. When I asked him why, he said, *"That's the name of it, Never Ending Road.* When I asked how long it is, he said *nobody knows."*

Maria's mouth dropped open. "Oh, come on. Somebody must know."

Hardy shrugged. "That's the same thing I said. Then Seth told me a short story. Years ago, a local family left here in a covered wagon loaded with supplies. They planned to get to the end of the road, then return to let everybody know where the road goes and how long it is. But … their plan did not work."

Maria frowned. "So, what happened to them?"

"Nobody saw them after that." He turned his head toward her. "Let's turn right up here, onto that trail. There's something down there I want to show you."

"Oh, yeah? Like what?"

"Just follow and trust me. It's not far. You'll understand when we get there."

Minutes later, they dismounted near a watering hole off the trail. While the horses drank, Hardy pulled Maria next to him and gave her a long kiss. When he pulled back from her and smiled, her big eyes glared at him.

"Hardy, you tricked me into stopping here. I'm gonna get even." She locked her arms around his waist and pulled him tight. After a long, deep kiss, she stared at him. "So, take *that*, you beast. You're not the first man I ever kissed, just the absolute best."

He tipped his hat. "I'll take that any day."

With her hands on her hips, she leaned forward. "How'd you find this place? You brought someone here before?"

"Never. I saw the path last time we were out here and thought it might be a great place to kiss a gorgeous woman. So here we are, and it's all I hoped it would be."

Maria tipped her hat and swung into the saddle.

On the road again, Hardy felt energized. "Maria, let's go for a fast ride if you're up to it."

She dipped her head toward him. "Okay, cowboy. Let's shift these animals into high gear."

Hardy grinned and dug his heels into the horse. While he and Maria raced down Never-Ending Road, he would pass her, and she would pass him, laughing harder.

When they slowed to a walk, Maria pointed at the horses, then at Hardy and herself. Between heavy breaths, she said, "I think both horses and riders got a great workout."

Neither could stop grinning. They dismounted and led the horses on a leisurely walk toward home.

During the walk, conversation came easily. They held hands and discussed what life could be for them if they shared it with each other, committed to peace and happiness by putting the other one first. When the talking tapered, they glanced at each other and smiled.

No need for more words. Clasped hands transferred messages, and their silence brought what they had missed before; an understanding and a connection that exists beyond the scope of mere words.

The powerful silence treated them to deer, rabbits, coyotes, and groundhogs, a broad stream with a large pond that attracted beavers, muskrats, quail, ducks, turkeys, and geese.

At the barn, Hardy and Maria removed bits, bridles, saddles, and blankets and wiped down each horse. They fed them oats and hay and filled troughs with fresh, cold water from the old pitcher pump.

Hardy gave Maria a long, goodbye kiss and whispered something in her ear that brought tears. She bit her lip as he climbed aboard Melvin and rode away.

Chapter Twenty-One

On the following Sunday after church, Hardy and Maria walked along the edge of Mystique Creek. In a light and easy conversation, Maria asked him about his past life, what he enjoyed most and least.

Uneasy about telling her where he came from, Hardy gave awkward responses. *Letting her believe I'm some kind of freak is the last thing I need. Yet, lying or being evasive would be worse.*

The more questions she asked, the more concerned he became. She did not probe nor dig for information but seemed fascinated. He opened up to her with careful, gradual answers until she knew he came from another world in a future time period and told her he had never met people like the residents of Mystique.

When they reached the area where Hardy first saw Debra Watts, Maria's questions focused on that incident and on Debra.

Hardy answered Maria's questions, relieved she focused on someone other than him.

Though Maria did not attend the trial, she had ample sources of information from the Miller household. She said her stepfather believed in Hardy's innocence all along. Maria told Nelda she wanted to meet Hardy as soon as the trial ended.

Relieved to hear that, Hardy shared with her the moments when he believed he could not win. Seth's testimony shocked him. Hardy remembered little about the gunshot wound and nothing about how it happened. The wound left no scars or marks of any kind. He knew Seth would not lie. But how could anyone convince a jury that Hardy did not remember it?

He did not know and would not ask if Maria had heard about that part of Seth's testimony.

***

Hardy and Maria sat on big stones near the creekbank and talked for an hour. At one pause, she drew a deep breath.

"Hardy, the more I know about you, the more I care about you. I hope you feel the same about me."

"Oh, I do, Maria. I do. But I think you know me much better than I know you."

She caught his shirt and pulled him close. "Well, don't just sit there. Kiss me like you mean it."

After an hour or more near the now-famous landmark by the creek, Hardy and Maria started home. They stopped for an occasional kiss, and Hardy began to ask questions.

"Tell me, Maria, where you came from before you moved in with the Millers. Was it a lot like this place?"

She stopped and grabbed his hand. "It was *nothing* like this place, Hardy. You may not believe this, but I came from the same world you did. I can't recall where I lived, but it may have been the same time period you came from."

Hardy's mouth fell open. "What? Are you kidding me? Please don't say that just to make me feel better."

"I would never do that, but I was a bit afraid to tell you earlier. If you came here to escape from many things in your previous world, you might not want to associate with other people from there."

Hardy looked past her and led her to a pair of stumps shaded by large trees. He kissed her again, picked her up, and sat her gently on a stump. He sat on one near her and folded his hands.

"Maria, I'm glad I got away from that life. What I desperately need from that other world is you. You make my life complete, and you make me happier than I've e ever been. I'll tell you anything you want to know … if I can remember."

He stared at the ground, then looked up. "I believe you and I are together for a special reason."

She nodded. "Me too, Hardy. I know much more about this place than I remember about where I came from." She stood, stepped over to him, and took his hand. "I agree with you. A higher power put us together here. If we accept that, everything will go right for us. I truly believe that because I believe in you and *us*."

A small tear appeared on his cheek as he stood. "Maria, I need to tell you something I have never said to any woman in my lifetime."

She caught his waist and pulled him close. "I hope it's not something bad."

He gazed into her eyes. "I'll tell you, and you let me know if it's bad." He swallowed hard.

"I'm falling in love with you, Maria. If you're not ready for that, please don't pretend. I couldn't stand it. I couldn't handle a broken heart."

Maria let go of him. "Hardy, I'm twenty-two years old. I've waited a long time to hear those words from the right man, one who truly feels what he says. I believe you mean that, and it's all so special because … I love you, too. I really do."

On their way to town, they agreed the walk was much too short. "So strange," she said. "I feel like I'm dancing on clouds."

Hardy laughed. "That sounds funny, but I feel exactly the same like I could jump off a cliff, sail among the clouds and sweep you up in my arms."

They laughed and talked as they danced along and shared dreams of what their future together could become. Maria squeezed his hand and made a sudden stop. "What are we going to tell everybody? Should we say we are a couple? Should we tell everyone we know we're gonna get..." She stopped and shook her head. "Hardy, please tell me if I'm reading too much into this or if I'm going too fast with everything."

He stopped and grabbed her waist. "Maria, would you like to have a couple of kids with *Brooke* for their last name?"

Wide-eyed she looked up at him. "What does that mean? I don't know.... Hardy, is that a proposal? Do you want me to..."

He pulled her tight and whispered in her ear. "Maria, will you spend the rest of your life with a man who loves you more than life itself? Will you be my one and *only*? Will you marry me, Maria?"

Chapter Twenty-Two

A week flew by since Maria heard those precious words from Hardy. While the minister delivered his Sunday morning sermon, Maria trembled in the pew beside Nelda. A tear ran down her cheek.

Nelda grabbed Maria's hand and whispered, "Everything will be all right. Worrying solves nothing."

Maria whispered, "I can't help it. Something must be wrong." She saw people staring, excused herself, and walked out.

After the service, Max and Nelda stopped at the bench out front where Maria waited and cried. They eased her up and Nelda hugged her.

"Maria, Max and I will take you over to Hardy's apartment, and you can knock on the door. If he's home, you can ask him what's wrong."

"I want to, but I'm afraid he'll be there and tell me he doesn't want to keep our date. Or maybe he doesn't want to see me anymore."

As they got into the carriage, Max squeezed Maria's hand. "He may not be feeling well, Maria. But whatever it is, we should go check on him."

Maria nodded. "This is so awkward, but I have to know if he's okay." She wiped another tear as Max drove the carriage across the street and parked in front of the store. At the staircase, Max stepped aside and beckoned for Maria to get in front. "You have to be first."

Maria's legs shook as she climbed the stairs. She stopped at the door, drew a heavy breath, and gave a gentle knock. After a few seconds with no response, Max reached around her and pounded on the door. A few seconds later, Max called out, "Hey, Hardy. Max Miller here. Are you there? Are you okay?" Again, he pounded on the door. No response.

Minutes after at the carriage, Max shook his head while Nelda folded her hands in silent prayer, and Maria cried. Max caught Maria's shoulders.

"Listen to me, little lady, we'll get to the bottom of this, but you have to talk to me. Earlier, you said the Walkers would not be at church because today is their anniversary, and they were taking the day off. Is that what they said to you? Or did someone else tell you?"

She wiped her eyes and looked up at him. "That's what Hardy told me last Friday. I haven't talked to him since. He said the Walkers are taking a day for themselves. They're going out for a long, romantic ride. But Hardy said he would meet me at church. And … well, you know the rest."

Max rubbed his chin. "Did Hardy say where they would be going for their ride?"

Maria sniffled. "No. I'm not sure if they told him."

"Hardy didn't tell you about any other plans he had for today?"

With a fast headshake, she stared up at him. "Absolutely not. We talked about our date for this afternoon, and he said he's looking forward to dinner at your house and our horseback ride afterward."

Max looked at Maria and Nelda. "Okay, you two wait here for a couple of minutes. I'm going to look around. Try to think of anything else Hardy may have said about today. Anything at all."

Max climbed the fence into the back yard.

In less than ten minutes, Max climbed back over the fence. He stopped in front of Nelda and Maria.

"Ladies, I don't know the best way to say this, but something doesn't seem right here. The Walkers usually keep their mule and the store wagon in the back yard. I didn't see either one. There's likely a good reason for that, but I need to find out."

After a quick meal, Max and Maria saddled the two riding horses and headed for the Walkers' home. They found wagon tracks, carriage tracks, and hoof prints, but none appeared fresh.

Chickens squawked and scattered when Max and Maria approached the Walkers' home. Max swung off the saddle and looked at Maria.

"Nobody's home. The dog's not barking." He stepped onto the porch. "But we'll see what happens." He knocked on the door, stepped down, and checked the small carriage house.

"Empty," he announced. "That means we find and follow carriage tracks."

They followed the trail through the woods behind the Walker's home. With too many previous tracks, the fresh carriage tracks became tough to find, but the riders used their best guesses and kept moving.

They followed the same trail for several minutes. Max stopped his horse and checked his pocket watch. "Maria, we've been following this trail for almost half-an-hour." He cupped his hands and called out for Wayne. He waited and called again. Still no answer.

Maria sat on her horse and listened while Max called twice more. With no reply, they started again and followed the same trail. When the horses stopped to relieve themselves, Maria shaded her eyes and looked down the trail among the scattered trees. In the distance, something looked unusual. With a smile on her lips, she pointed ahead.

"Mister Miller, do you see what I see?"

He looked where she pointed. "I see something that looks unusual, but from here, I can't tell what it is."

Maria leaned toward him and pointed again. "Do you see where another trail cuts off to the right up there? Follow that trail with your eyes till you see a very large tree, then look up."

He found the big tree, and smiled. "That looks like a tree house."

Max rode up beside her "I see it now. Let's ride over there. I bet we find a carriage parked nearby."

A dog barked as they stopped their horses under the tree. Someone above yelled, "No matter what we do, we can't hide." Wayne laughed as the two below looked up.

Max wore a large grin. "Wayne, we hate to bother you and Wanda on your anniversary, but we need to talk. Can you come down, please?"

With Wayne and Wanda on the ground, Max told them about Hardy while Maria cried. Wanda gasped when Max said he could not find the wagon or mule.

Wayne stared into the distance while he rubbed his chin. "I can't believe this. It makes no sense. Hardy made a solemn promise that…"

At home a half-hour later, Max and Maria traded their horses for the carriage. They would meet the Walkers at the huge barn across from the railroad track.

"I'm not superstitious," Wayne said as the carriages approached the big, open door, "but this makes me nervous."

They stopped just inside the door and stared at a mule munching hay in a stall.

Wayne yelled, "That's Melvin, my mule."

Melvin's ears perked. Wanda's eyes filled with tears as she cried out, "Oh, Hardy, what have you done? We loved you and trusted you so much." She turned to Wayne. "You think he's gone back to his old world?"

Wayne gritted his teeth. "I don't know if he made it there, but it certainly looks like he tried again. I can't believe this. It's unreal in more ways than one. But if he didn't make it, he must be here somewhere. I'm gonna look around."

Maria shook her head and walked outside. "I'll look out here."

Wayne followed Max through the barn and opened the huge rear door. Max's mouth fell open. "This looks like your wagon."

With anger in his voice, Wayne replied, "Yeah, it's mine, all right." He took slow steps toward the wagon and looked over the sideboard. His head jerked back. "Oh, my God."

Max stepped to the wagon and looked in. Like Wayne, Max jerked his head. "Is that…?"

Wayne lowered the wagon's tailgate and hopped in. Max followed. Someone lay near the rear corner, with blood on the wagon floor near his head. A pale-faced Wayne turned toward Max. "It's Hardy. Give me a hand, please. We have to check him out."

Max removed his expensive hat and put his ear to Hardy's chest. "The heartbeat sounds pretty strong to me. His breath is kinda ragged, so he may be feeling a lot of pain. Let's grab some clean rags, wipe the blood from his face, and try to get him out of here."

From the wagon, Wayne cupped his hands around his mouth and yelled, "Wanda, bring some clean rags from the carriage. Hurry. Hardy's bleeding."

Wanda jumped and ran to the carriage, passing Maria without speaking. Maria followed her and screamed, "What's wrong?"

Wanda turned away from the carriage with a handful of rags, shouting while she ran. "They found Hardy in the wagon, and he's bleeding."

Chapter Twenty-Three

Doctor Tebo stepped from the treatment room into the waiting area of his clinic. Maria sprang off the bench.

"Doctor, is my boyfriend okay? His name is Hardy."

The doctor raised his hand. "Sit down, please." He looked at Max, Nelda, Wayne, Wanda and again at Maria. "I have good news for everybody. I believe your friend has a good chance for a complete recovery. But it may take a while. He has a concussion, and he suffered cuts and bruises on his left arm and hand. I cleaned and bandaged all the wounds."

He looked again at the people in the room. "Looks like a bad fall. Can anyone tell me what caused this?"

The four people shook their heads, no. "None of us were there when it happened."

Maria waved her hand. "Doctor, can we take him home now? We can make sure he gets lots of rest."

"Sorry, Maria, he needs to stay here in the clinic for at least three days. I should know more by then. You can come by and see him any day you like, but please limit your visits to about twenty minutes. Rest is quite critical."

"Will he know who I am?" Maria asked.

"It's hard to say, young lady. It's likely he'll have some temporary memory loss, at least for a few days. But don't give up on him. His memory will likely return in bits and pieces over a period of weeks, maybe months."

Four long days later, Maria hitched her horse in front of the general store. Finding no customers inside, she grabbed

Wanda's arm and whispered, "I just came from the clinic, and I need to talk to both of you. Can we sit, please?"

Wayne's face grew pale. "Is everything okay? Is Hardy…"

Maria's hand shook. "A few minutes ago, I went to see him. But the doctor wouldn't let me talk to him until I talked to you two. He said Hardy may be okay to come home tomorrow. That's the good news. He also said his memory is returning faster than expected."

Wanda grinned. "We're happy to hear that, but you seem upset. What's going on?"

Maria stood and looked back and forth at Wayne and Wanda. "The doctor told me Hardy remembered what happened and told him that a man had come to his apartment early on Sunday morning. The man had a big club, and he hit Hardy on the back of the head. Hardy doesn't remember anything after that, but he remembers the man who hit him."

Wayne and Wanda gasped. "Oh, my God. Who was it?"

Maria's face grew white. "The doctor wouldn't say. He wants me to bring at least two other people to the clinic and ask Hardy to repeat what he said earlier. Of course, I wanted you two to be there. I also want Max and Nelda, but they're at home, and I don't want to wait any longer."

Within three minutes, Wayne and Wanda secured all entrances to their business. Five minutes after, they stepped out of the carriage and into the clinic. Maria tied her horse to the hitching post.

Dr. Tebo looked through his window, and opened the door. He locked it again after they entered.

"I don't want anybody else coming in until we're done here. We'll go in and talk to Hardy. I hope he tells you the same thing he told me earlier. So let me start the conversation, please."

Hardy sat up when the three entered. "Hello, Wayne and Wanda, and my Princess." He extended his hand to Wayne and then to Wanda. He gave his hand to Maria but did not let go. He smiled and then frowned and said the smile hurt his face.

The doctor cleared his throat. "Hardy, I'm glad your friends are here. You're recuperating much faster than I expected. Would you please tell these people what you told me earlier today?"

Hardy's face looked blank. "Sorry, I forgot what we talked about."

The doctor leaned closer. "Just tell them what you told me this morning about someone coming to your home last Sunday."

"I remember that we talked, but I don't remember what we talked *about*. What was it?"

Maria squeezed his hand and leaned toward him. "Hardy, tell us what you told the doctor. Was it …?"

"No, no, no," the doctor cut in. "You can tell us another time, Hardy."

Over the next few minutes, Hardy talked of many things that seemed disconnected. Doctor Tebo cut in. "Sorry, visitor time has ended." He looked at the other three people in the room. "Please say your goodbyes. We'll set up a time for tomorrow or the next day." He turned to Maria. "I'm sorry, my dear. I need to keep Hardy here for another day or two. Could be longer."

Wayne and Wanda said goodbye to Hardy and waited by the door. Maria turned toward him, squeezed his hand again, and wiped a tear from her eye. "I'll come back tomorrow, Hardy. Please remember I love you so much."

He wiped his own tear. "I promise I won't forget, Maria. I love you, too. If you have time tomorrow, I want to tell you what happened to me. How I got this big bruise on the back of my head."

He released her hand. Dead silence filled the room.

"Oh, Hardy. You can tell me now. It's okay." Maria turned to the others.

"It's okay, Hardy," Doctor Tebo said.

Maria took his hand again. "So, my dear, tell me everything."

Hardy told them a man banged on his door one morning, but he couldn't remember which day. "I was getting dressed, and before I got to the door, I heard someone going downstairs. I saw a man at the bottom with his back toward me., and I yelled, *Hello*. I went down the steps. When I reached him, he turned around and lifted a big club. I started to run up the stairs, but he hit me. That's the last thing I remember."

"Hardy, you told me the man's name," Dr. Tebo said. He nodded at Maria. "Tell her, please."

Hardy rubbed the back of his head, groaned, and then jerked his hand away. "Oh, it was, uhm" His face grew blank again. "I'm sorry. I know who it was, but I can't think of his name right now."

Maria turned. "Doctor Tebo, if I arrange a good place for Hardy to recuperate, can he go home today?"

"Well, little lady, he lives alone and has to climb stairs. That could be risky until he's had more time to heal."

"I understand, and I don't want to risk his recovery, but I think I can make arrangements that would be ideal for him. I'll try to get here this afternoon to let you know."

156

Later, Maria and Nelda returned to the clinic. They assured Doctor Tebo Hardy would be safe and comfortable in their home, with no stairs except for the porch, and the ladies could take good care of him.

"You have my consent, but I need to stop by to check on him every couple of days."

Nelda and Maria left the clinic with Hardy and two large pillows in the carriage but stopped at Hardy's apartment and picked up Hardy's pillow, the one he must have to sleep well.

At the carriage, Wayne and Wanda wished Hardy a speedy recovery.

Hardy grinned. "Thank you. I'll be glad when I can go to my own home. But I know these two ladies will take great care of me until then."

"If you like, we'll go through your apartment to make sure all is okay before you move back in," Wanda said.

"Yes, thank you. Yesterday at the clinic, I stayed awake for a long time, thinking about what the doctor told me. He said you found me in the bed of your wagon at that old barn. Is that true?"

"Yes," Wayne said.

Hardy's chin dropped. "I hope you didn't think I tried to go to my old world again. I don't remember much about it, but I know I *never* want to return."

Wanda wiped a tear. "Sorry, Hardy, that crossed my mind when we found you there."

"I'm sorry too, Hardy," Wayne said. "We were both upset about that. Forgive us?"

"You're both very special to me, and I kept my promise.," Hardy said. "No hard feelings."

***

In the General Store, Maria stopped at the counter and looked around. "Hello, anybody here?"

"Yes, my love, I'm right here."

She whirled. "Hardy, what are you doing up there? The doctor said *no ladders* for a month or longer, just in case."

"I know. This is a stepstool, barely a couple feet tall. Besides, the dizzy spells are almost gone, and no more headaches. It's been almost three weeks since I got whacked on the head."

He stepped down, looked at the bag Maria left on the counter, and rubbed his belly. "Did you bring enough for both of us?"

"Sure, I did." She opened the bag and pulled out a pair of dirty, worn-out gloves. "Which one would you like?"

Hardy's face wrinkled. "I thought my sweet girlfriend might have brought lunch for the two of us." He rubbed his belly again. "I'm hungry."

"Max sent me here to get a couple pairs of new gloves and sent the old pair to make sure I get the right kind and size. He's got huge hands."

Hardy sighed and stepped behind the counter. He opened the glove drawer, pulled out two new pairs, and laid them on the counter.

"Max buys gloves here all the time, and he always wants the same kind." Hardy grinned as he picked up the old gloves and dropped them into the trashcan. "Wanna go to the café? I'll buy lunch if you'll go get it."

She shook her head. "I'm hungry too, but I'd rather eat what I brought for us. It's in the carriage. We can sit out there and eat while I tell you what Max wants you to know."

"Sounds great, but sorry, Maria. I have to stay inside until Wayne gets here, and I don't know when that will be."

"Well, I do."

His face puzzled. "Yeah?"

"Yeah. I saw him on the way here. He should be here in about ten minutes."

Hardy laughed. "Seems like you're always one step ahead of me."

"Make that *three* steps." Maria smirked.

While Hardy and Maria enjoyed lunch in the carriage, she said, "Nelda, and I liked having you in our home, and we miss you."

Hardy smiled. "You two took excellent care of me. You can't know how much I appreciate it, and I've never had better meals anywhere. I miss it also, and I miss *you*. But I'm glad to be home. Understand?"

"I do, but I hope someday you and I will have our home together. Do *you understand?*"

He kissed her. "I do indeed."

A smile on her face, Maria cleared her throat and picked up her papers. "And now, down to business. I have to refer to these notes I made early this morning. Don't want to miss anything Max said to tell you. I can't mention the suspect's name. It might cause *undue influence*. Whatever that means."

"Okay, I'm ready."

Maria breathed deep. "Max got the search warrant a few days ago. He took two guards and the blacksmith with him and went to the suspect's home early one morning. As you can guess, the suspect was not glad to see him and tried to slam the door shut when he saw who was there. But Sam kicked it open, and Max arrested the man."

Hardy stroked his chin. "What did he charge him with?"

"He didn't say, and I didn't ask. But he wants you to write down all you can remember about the man you suspect and bring the paper with you to the trial."

"That won't take long to write. I don't remember anything after he clubbed me until I woke up in the clinic."

"He knows that Hardy. But he also wants you to jot down all the times you saw the man before that happened and what he said. Max wants to show the suspect's motive for what he did to you."

She glanced at her notes again. "Max will be the prosecutor. Someone suggested Seth as judge. Max didn't agree or disagree but may select someone else. No jury yet."

Hardy swallowed the last of his drink. "I'll bet the defendant hides out somewhere and never shows up for the trial."

"That would surprise *me*."

"Why is that?"

"He's been locked in the chicken coop jail since the day Max arrested him. The guards untie his hands when he's eating, which is twice a day, or when he's in the outhouse."

Hardy and Maria slapped hands with each other and laughed together.

Chapter Twenty-Four

Hardy looked around the courtroom. With his hands tied behind him, Luther Watts sat on the same chair Hardy had occupied. Hardy looked around again, searching the crowd in the room. He saw no other member of the Watts family. A broad grin crossed his face. His chest swelled.

Pastor Quake rapped the gavel. "Luther Watts, I am the acting judge for this trial, and I am informing you that the village of Mystique has charged you with stealing another person's property. Stand and tell the court how you wish to plead."

Luther stood and wagged his head. "I am not guilty of that. And I didn't break any other law."

Quake checked his paper again. "Luther Watts, you are also charged with assault and battery, with intent to do great bodily harm. How do you plead to that charge?"

"I told you. I am not guilty of anything. I don't break the law."

"You are also charged with attempted murder. What is your plea to that charge?"

Luther swung his head from side to side. "Not guilty. I broke no laws of any kind."

"You may be seated, Mister Watts."

Quake nodded at the prosecutor. "Present your case, Mister Miller."

Max stood, leaned forward, and glared at the defendant. "Mister Watts, do you remember Hardy Brooke, the man you tried to prosecute in this courtroom a few weeks ago? The same innocent man you stole money from and punched in the mouth after you tied his hands behind him?"

Luther jumped to his feet. "I never did anything like that. He slung his fist at me *first*."

The judge rapped his gavel. "Mister Miller, I assume you know remarks of that sort are not permitted in this courtroom."

"My apologies, Your Honor. I call Hardy Brooke, the victim of this horrible crime, to the witness chair."

After the oath, Max stopped near the stage and looked at Hardy. "Mister Brooke, please tell the court what some lowlife did to you a few weeks ago." He turned and stared at Luther Watts.

Quake rapped the gavel again. "Mister Miller, I will say this with a calm voice but only once—no more of those tactics in my courtroom. Whatever happened in previous trials has no bearing on this one, and I was not the judge for that last case. Do you understand?"

Max bowed his head. "My apologies, Your Honor." He spread his arms wide. "It will not be easy for me, but I will restrain myself from now on."

He turned again toward Hardy. "Mister Brooke, please tell our jury what happened to you on a Sunday morning a few weeks back."

"Ladies and gentlemen, on that Sunday morning in March, I heard a loud knock on my door while I got dressed for church. I yelled, *"Give me a minute* "Then I heard someone walking down the stairs. When I opened the door a couple of minutes after, someone stood at the bottom of the stairs with his back toward me. I said *hello*. He didn't answer. I went down to see who it was, but when I reached him, he turned and held up a big club. I tried to run upstairs, but he hit me."

Max leaned toward Hardy. "The man who hit you, did you see his face?"

"Yes, I did, right before he hit me. It was Luther Watts."

Luther stood and yelled, "Objection."

The judge turned and scowled. "Sit down and stay quiet, Mister Watts. Or I'll tell the guard to put a gag on you."

Max smiled. "What happened next, Mr. Brooke?"

"I woke up in Dr. Tebo's clinic the next day with a severe head injury."

After a moment of silence, Max stepped closer to Hardy. "Mister Brooke, since that encounter with your intruder, have you noticed anything missing from your apartment?"

"Yes, sir, my prize alarm clock. Someone took it from the shelf in my room."

Max nodded at the judge. "Your Honor, I'm done with this witness but may want to call him again."

Luther stood. "Your Honor, if I may, I'd like to ask this witness a question."

"You may proceed, Mister Watts."

With his hands tied behind him, Luther Watts swaggered toward the witness, then stopped and stared at him.

"Mr. Brooke, a few weeks ago in this courtroom, we learned how much you hate our town. You stole a wagon and a mule and tried to escape to your world. Even the *mule* was smart enough to know better. But you forced him to make the wrong turn anyway. Then you took the coward's way out by jumping from the wagon when the mule went wild. You damaged the stolen wagon, returned to work three hours late, and promised your boss you would never do that again. But you did it again. You damaged the wagon again, wound up with a serious injury, then tried to cover up everything by blaming it all on me and—"

Quake rapped the gavel and yelled, "That's enough, Mister Watts. You told me you had a question for this witness. I have heard none. Ask a question or close your mouth and sit down."

Luther bowed. "Very well, Your Honor. My apologies."

"Mister Brooke, since you hate this town, can't you buy a horse and ride Never Ending Road beyond the turnaround?"

Hardy started to reply. Luther cut in.

"No further questions, Your Honor."

The plaintiff moved to another chair on the stage while Max called Maria Miller to testify. Maria explained about Hardy missing their date and how the Miller family and the Walkers went looking for Hardy and found him in the wagon at the old barn.

Maria wiped her tears. "He was unconscious and bleeding from the back of his head. I was so afraid he would die before we got him to the clinic."

Max extended his hand toward Maria. "Thank you for your testimony." He turned again to the judge. "Your Honor, I am finished with this witness at this time."

Before Maria stepped down, the judge granted Luther the right to question her.

Luther stood and smirked. "Miss Maria, can we assume Hardy Brooke is your boyfriend?"

"Objection," Max yelled. "Immaterial."

The judge rapped the gavel. "Overruled. It may be pertinent."

Luther snickered and looked at Maria. "Is Hardy Brooke your boyfriend?"

"Yes, he is, and I am so proud of him."

"We didn't see you in this courtroom, Miss Maria, when your boyfriend was being tried for indecency with a child. So can we assume you know about your boyfriend's first attempt to escape to his former world? A witness in this courtroom testified not long ago that Mister Brooke stole that same wagon and mule and drove to the same barn where you found him this time. Do you know about his serious injuries when he wrecked the wagon? Do you know he betrayed the people he worked for, the people who trusted him?"

Maria shook her head. "He told me about that, but he also promised the Walkers he would never try it again."

"Yeah, but he lied," Luther snarled. "Your sweetheart broke his promise, wrecked the wagon again, and got hurt worse than the first time. Now he tries to cover for himself and blames it all on me, though I was nowhere around. You call that an honest boyfriend?"

Maria stood. "Hardy is a good, honest man and —"

Luther jerked his head toward the judge and shouted, "No further questions, Your Honor."

Max called Mrs. Walker, who told the jury how she and her husband inspected Hardy's room after the assault and found the prized alarm clock was missing. She described the stolen clock and gave Max a drawing, who placed it on the jury table, went down the steps, and turned to them.

"Ladies and gentlemen of the jury, Wanda Walker told me how her sister made a detailed drawing of that clock many years ago. When I went to Luther Watts' home with three other witnesses to arrest him, I took the drawing with me."

Max turned, pulled a clock from a bag near the front of the stage, and placed it on the table next to the drawing. "That is the clock I found on a shelf in Mister Watts' home."

Wide-eyed jurors nodded while they compared the drawing to the clock.

Maxwell Miller beamed as he turned to the judge. "Your Honor, I have finished my questions for this witness."

The judge turned. "Your witness, Mister Watts. Any questions?"

Luther stood. "Yes, Your Honor."

The judge lowered his head at him. "You may proceed, Mister Watts, as long as you remember to respect this court and the people in it."

Luther walked closer to the witness and stopped in front of her. "Mrs. Walker, how long would you say that clock's been in your family?"

"About thirty years."

"Thirty years? So, we can assume the company that made that clock had been in business for a while before that. Does that seem reasonable?"

"I suppose."

Luther nodded. "It may have been a lot longer, but do you assume they made only one clock like the one here? It seems a lot more likely they made hundreds, maybe thousands of clocks exactly like the one here. You may have had one like my mother's clock. Drawings?" He shook his head. "No, I don't have any. But that clock's been in *my* family for over thirty-*five* years and on my fireplace mantle for more than ten."

Luther frowned at the judge. "No more questions, Your Honor."

After a one-hour break to feed faces, the judge rapped his gavel again while a new arrival took a seat in the audience. Hardy jerked his head around. He looked at the man again and recognized Jody Watts.

Max called Wayne Walker to the stand. Wayne told the jury how he and his wife followed the wagon tracks and horseshoe prints from Hardy's apartment out to the road and all the way to the big barn where they found the wagon. Wayne pulled a paper from his pocket and gave it to Max.

"Mister Prosecutor, my wife drew copies of the tracks we saw. That drawing shows the shoe prints of the mule that pulled the wagon, along with the wagon tracks, and another set of horseshoe prints. That last set of prints is on top of the mule prints, which proves the horse was behind the mule. An extra horse tied behind the wagon would give the driver return transportation after leaving the wagon and mule at the barn."

Wayne stared at Luther Watts. "This crime was not spontaneous. It was well planned."

He waved the drawing above his head. "When you look closely at this, you can see a distinct mark in the horse's left front shoe print. That mark is an arrowhead."

Max nodded. "That's good, solid evidence someone other than Hardy Brooke drove that wagon from his apartment to the barn." He laid the drawing on the jury's table and waited while the jurors studied the illustration. When they finished, Max turned to the judge.

"Your Honor, I have no more questions for this witness."

The judge turned to Luther. "Mister Watts, do you have questions for this witness?"

"I have no questions for him, Your Honor. But I have no idea what the witness means by that fancy mark on a horseshoe. It don't prove anything *to* me or *about* me."

Max smiled. "Your Honor, with your permission and the consent of Mister Jody Watts, I would like him to take the witness chair. I want to ask a few questions."

Chapter Twenty-Five

Max turned toward Jody Watts. "I have some very simple questions about your family. If that's okay, please take the witness chair."

Jody Watts stood, and walked to the witness chair. His face stayed puzzled as he swore to tell the truth.

Max stood in front of his witness. "Thank you, Mister Watts. I have no interest in making you feel uncomfortable. I want to ask a couple of easy questions. Just relax, please."

"I'd like to ask about your parents. Can you tell us if your mother or father kept a favorite treasured item at home? Something that stayed in the family for a long time, like a book, a clock, or musical instrument?"

Jody grinned. "If they left anything like that, it would likely be in my house now. Both parents are gone, but I live in the home I grew up in."

"So, Mister Watts, you have nothing in your home they left behind?"

"Nothing but an old rocking chair. I would never part with that. But my mother's friend gave her a violin, and Mom promised herself many times she would learn to play it."

Max leaned forward. "And did she learn?"

Jody shook his head. "It's kinda sad. She picked it up several times but never learned to play a single tune."

"Did that violin get passed along in the family? Is it a favorite keepsake?"

"I wish that was the case." Jody fidgeted in the chair. "But I don't know what happened to it. Haven't seen it in many years. Our family was never very good with keepsakes, anyway."

"Thank you for sharing that, Mister Watts. Anything else your family may have kept through the years and passed along, like a family bible or alarm clock?"

"I doubt it. I think I would remember if there was anything else."

"Thank you. I have a couple more questions, and we'll let you step down. Can you estimate how often you've been in your brother Luther's house over the years?"

Jody leaned forward, his face blank, his eyes wide. "Well … I couldn't hazard a guess, but lots of times."

"Do you know if your brother kept anything in his house that might be considered a family heirloom? Or anything passed along in the family?"

"Nothing I can think of."

Max walked to the jury table and picked up the clock. "Mister Watts, have you ever seen this clock?"

"I don't think so."

Max held the clock high. "Mister Jody Watts, are you telling us you never saw this clock in your parent's house or brother's house?"

"It's a handsome clock, but I'm quite sure I've never seen it anywhere."

Max returned the clock to the table and brought another item from the bag.

"How about this, Mister Watts?" Max held up the item. "Ever seen this before?"

The witness stared. Color filled his face. He did not answer.

"All I'm asking for, Mister Watts, is a yes or no. Please tell us if you've seen this item before?"

Jody Watts nodded.

Max looked at the jury, then around at the crowd, and back to the witness. "Mister Watts, to clarify the court record, we need a spoken word that means the same as your nod, please."

The witness nodded again. "Yes, I have."

Max pointed to different features as he described what he held. "It has a handle at the bottom and a much larger striking part at the top. It appears to be custom-made for a specific purpose. Tell us what you call this, please, Mister Watts."

"It's uhh ... a club."

Max nodded. "Yes, it certainly is. And a big one. Tell us where you've seen it, please."

Jody Watts looked around and crossed his legs. "It's for self-defense."

"Self-defense for who? Did you make this?"

"No, I did not."

"Did your brother make this? Do you often see this club in your brother's home?"

Jody turned to the judge. "Your Honor, I do not want to answer any more questions."

Max raised his hand. "Just one more question, Your Honor."

"Proceed, Mister Prosecutor. But I will not pressure the witness to answer."

Max held the club higher. "Jody, please tell us how many times you saw this in your brother's home."

He spread his hands. "I don't know."

"Thank you once again, Mister Watts. No more questions."

The judge turned to the defendant. "Mister Luther Watts, do you have any questions for this witness?"

Luther did not stand. He did not speak, but shook his head no and stared at the floor.

Max glanced at someone in the room, smiled, nodded, and called his next witness.

"Doctor Tebo, is Hardy Brooke one of your patients?"

"He is. I treated him for a serious head injury a few weeks ago."

Doctor, in your professional opinion, can you tell the jury what may have caused that injury?"

"Objection," Luther yelled as he leaped up from the chair, stumbled, and fell to one knee. A guard helped him to his feet, and he cried out again.

"Objection, Your Honor. The prosecutor is asking for opinions instead of facts."

Max raised his hand. "Your Honor, Dr. Tebo is a well-trained physician who has treated many head injuries in his practice. I believe he is well qualified to render a professional judgment for a head injury."

After the judge overruled the objection, Dr. Tebo stood and placed his hand on his head.

"A large, blunt instrument caused Mister Brooke's injury. I examined the sides and floor of the wagon where his friends found him. I saw a fair amount of blood on the wagon floor where his head had been. I found no blunt objects in or near the wagon that could have caused the injury."

Max handed the club to the doctor. "Tell us, Dr. Tebo, could this have caused Mister Hardy Brooke's head injury?"

The doctor examined the club. "This has the right size, shape, and weight to cause the kind of injury Mister Brooke suffered. Also, I see some blood soaked into the wood here on the big end. This is quite likely the weapon that caused the injury."

Max took the weapon from the doctor, placed it on the table, and told the jury, "This is the weapon I found in Luther Watts' home the day I arrested him."

He turned to the witness. "Thank you, Dr. Tebo. No more questions."

The judge turned to Luther. "Your witness, Mister Watts."

In slow motion, Luther stood, keeping his feet apart. He cleared his throat while he walked over to face the witness.

"Dr. Tebo, have you been to Hardy Brooke's room above the general store?"

"Yes, the day after I admitted Mister Brooke to my clinic."

"You must have seen the stairs we've heard so much about. Isn't it possible for someone to fall backward down those stairs and get a head injury like the one you described?"

"Yes, it is. That's why I went. I looked carefully at the steps. None appeared damaged. I found blood only on the bottom step and none inside the apartment. Mister Brooke's injury occurred near that bottom step, but his friends found him in the wagon with his head near the tailgate."

"So, you choose to believe Mr. Brooke could not drive the wagon to the barn after he fell down the stairs?"

"Highly unlikely. That type of injury renders a person unconscious immediately, not an hour later. Regardless of how his injury occurred, it happened before the trip to the barn, not after. Mr. Brooke could never climb into that wagon after the injury, drive the wagon three or four miles to the barn, and leave no trace of blood near the driver's seat. I found blood in the wagon only near the tailgate. I also treated deep scratches on Mr. Brooke's back. I'm convinced someone hit him on the head and dragged him into the wagon."

Luther stared at the doctor until the judge interrupted. "Mister Watts, if you have no more questions for this witness, please be seated."

Max extended his hand toward the blacksmith. "Your Honor, I would like to call Sam Smith as a witness."

Sam carried a small bag to the witness chair. Max took the paper from the jury table and handed it to the blacksmith.

"Sam, Wanda Walker made that drawing from horseshoe prints that led from Hardy Brooke's home to the giant barn we discussed today. Please tell the jury what you know."

Sam nodded, smiled, and held up the paper. "This is a drawing of a unique horseshoe design for a shoe I made in my shop several times."

"For how many horses, Sam?"

Sam smiled. "One."

"Mr. Smith, please tell the jury the story behind that horseshoe."

Luther jumped up. "Objection."

The judge wrinkled his face. "Based on what, Mr. Watts?"

"Nobody wants to hear a boring story. It's a waste of time, and I'm tired of sitting in that chair."

Max held up his hand. "Your Honor, It's a very interesting short story."

Judge Quake nodded. "Proceed, Mr. Smith."

Sam pulled the horseshoe from the bag and held it up. "The arrowhead that points forward at the front shows up in the hoof print. I created this shoe exactly the way my customer wanted for a horse I've shoed many times."

Max grinned. "Sam, please tell the jury about that horse."

"The owner of this horse is left-handed. This shoe is for the left front hoof of a horse named *Lefty*. The other feet get standard shoes."

Max nodded. "And tell the jury, Sam, who owns the horse that gets the special shoe."

Sam nodded. "Lefty's a great horse. He belongs to Luther Watts."

Max took the note and held it up. "Below this drawing is a sworn affidavit from Mrs. Wanda Walker that she made this drawing from the hoof prints left in front of Hardy Brooke's home on September twenty-first of this year."

"Mister Watts, would you explain to the jury how this hoof print appeared at that place on that date?"

Luther stood and looked around the courtroom. "The only thing I'll explain is ... I'm being framed. The prosecutor should be ashamed of himself."

Chapter Twenty-Six

Saturday morning, the day following the trial, the news reporter stood next to Hardy and Maria in the crowd that gathered to watch Luther Watts' punishment. The reporter handed his notebook to Hardy.

"Check this, please, and see if it needs anything before it goes to press this afternoon. I'll take notes today and add to it before I submit it."

Maria moved close, looked up at Hardy and whispered. "He probably knows it all already. He was in the courtroom every day."

Hardy did not want to discuss the trial with anyone but took the notebook and read the reporter's entry. Hardy returned the notebook. "Looks good to me."

***

On Friday, October 21, the jury lost no time rendering a verdict after Maxwell Miller rested the prosecution's case in the Brooke/Watts trial.

The full-house crowd clapped and shouted approval while Luther Watts stood and shouted obscenities, and Judge Quake hammered the gavel several times.

The following morning, a large crowd gathered near Never Ending Road to watch the penalty crew carry out the sentence. Some onlookers discussed the last time they saw this maximum penalty enforced, nearly 29 years ago.

***

Luther Watts stood bound and gagged while a crew member read him his right to choose.

"Luther Watts, you will be addressed as Convict Watts since you no longer deserve the consideration of Sir or Mister. You will nod to accept a sentence or shake your head to reject a sentence. You cannot reject all sentences. If you do not fully cooperate, this crew will decide your fate. Do you understand?"

Watts nodded.

"Convict Watts, among other crimes, you have been found guilty of attempted murder. For the penalty of that crime, do you prefer to face a firing squad which will, *here and now*, result in your immediate death?" Five crew members held up rifles and waited.

Luther's eyes grew wide again. His Adam's apple bulged. He shook his head.

"Convict Watts, instead of execution, do you prefer to be forever banished from this life and sentenced to travel beyond the turnaround point on Never Ending Road?"

The convict nodded.

Following a ten-minute break, the Speaker for the Punishment Crew stood beneath the Never Ending Road sign and faced the crowd. On his right, stood the convict, his hands tied behind him, the gag still in place.

On the Speaker's left stood a large, white, horse, his head high, wearing an expensive, hand-tooled leather saddle and bridal. The Speaker caught the bridle as he lifted the bullhorn.

"Ladies and gentlemen, your attention, please. During our short break, the members of the crew agreed, with a unanimous decision, that the victim of this crime deserves a bit of restitution. We have awarded the criminal's prize horse, *Lefty*, to the victim, Hardy Brooke."

Luther's face distorted. His bulging eyes teared, his body shook while the crowd exploded. People laughed, cheered, whistled, clapped, and screamed "Yes" and "Alright."

The speaker raised his bullhorn again. "If anyone here feels justified in saying something to this convict, step forward now."

As the cheering and clapping died, many people looked around. With angled heads, they whispered while they searched for the Watts family. They found…none.

When the Speaker raised the bullhorn to proceed, Hardy threw up his hand.

"Mister Speaker, I would like to express my true feelings for that convict. Please remove his gag."

"Very well, Mister Brooke. Step forward."

Hardy led Maria to the front of the crowd, let go of her hand, and stared at the convict. After a long, large grin, Hardy yelled, "Luther *Low Life* Watts, this is the first time I've been happy to see you. I have just one comment to make."

Hardy's right fist tightened. His right arm quivered while muscles bulged from his shoulder to his wrist. He leaned back and then threw himself forward and slammed a roundhouse punch. Hardy heard and felt the split in Luther's upper lip, the crunching gristle in the man's nose, and watched blood splatter over the lowlife's face as he fell backward. The man's head struck solid ground with a loud thump.

Hardy stepped forward, stood over him, looked down into wide eyes, and grinned.

"Just a parting gift, Luther. Enjoy your trip."

Hardy picked up Maria, sat her on Lefty, and led him away while the crowd cheered, clapped, and yelled.

Outside the crowd, he and Maria turned and looked back. Two crew members brought another horse, tied the convict's hands in front of him and helped him into the saddle. Three guards with rifles ready would escort Luther Watts down Never Ending Road to the no-return point and watch him cross the line. With their job finished, they would turn and head home.

Chapter Twenty-Seven

Hardy swallowed hard while he looked in the mirror and knew he would never be the same person from this day forward. After today, the past would not matter.

His new, tailor-made suit made him look taller. He did not care. Today would be the most special day of his life. Once more, he smiled at himself in the mirror, danced down the stairs, and started for the church.

Three or four people had offered him a ride to the church for this event, but Hardy wanted to walk. He could think much better while he walked and wanted no conversation with anyone on his way there.

He remembered wondering what this day would be like when *and if* it finally came. That day had arrived, and it felt nothing like he'd imagined.

He looked across the street in total surprise at the crowd in front of the church and wondered why they were not inside where it was likely cooler.

From yesterday's short rehearsal, Hardy knew to stay by the minister behind the curtain on the church stage until the ceremony started. Hardy would not see Maria that day until she walked down the aisle to meet him.

He grew a bit nervous as he walked through the church's rear door, wishing he and Maria had decided to marry with only a minister present. But, like most brides, Maria wanted a crowd. Hardy took a deep breath and told himself she was entitled to have a proper ceremony with lots of people.

He jumped when Reverend Quake spoke behind him. "Hello. Good to see you, Hardy. Ready for your big day?"

Hardy chuckled. "Yes sir, as ready as I'll ever be, I guess."

The minister slapped him on the shoulder. "Everything will be fine. It takes only a few minutes, so relax."

The rear church door opened and closed as someone stepped inside. "Well, I see the groom is here. Hello, Hardy. You look like you're ready for this."

Hardy turned. "Wayne, I'm so happy you're here. Thanks for being the Best Man."

Wayne grinned. "I've always been the best man." He laughed hard. "Just kidding, Hardy. I'm happy for you and flattered to be asked."

The piano player began. While the curtain opened, the minister motioned for Hardy and Wayne. "Okay, guys, it's time. Follow me down the stairs."

Halfway to the altar, Hardy stopped, his mouth open as he stared at the crowd. He saw no empty seats in the church, and the open front doors revealed many more people outside.

To Hardy, it seemed mere seconds passed until the ceremony began. Maria had revealed nothing to him about her bridal party except that she selected only one bridesmaid.

Now, Hardy wore a huge grin as the bridesmaid marched down the aisle with a beautiful bouquet. He recalled the last time she walked down an aisle toward him and delivered her critical, courageous testimony in the courthouse.

But today, Debra Watts wore a big smile, obviously proud to participate in the ceremony. She had blossomed into a beautiful young lady. She took her place, and whispered, "Hello, Hardy. Great to see you."

The music changed to a lively tune, and everyone in the audience stood to watch the next person in the wedding. Hardy's mouth fell open. A lump formed in his throat, and tears wet his eyes while a beautiful lady who had become his best friend came down the aisle toward him. He drew a deep, ragged breath and whispered, "Maria, I love you more than anything."

***

Hardy appreciated all the people who attended the wedding, all the gifts, the well-wishers, and the huge reception at the café. Tired of it all, he just wanted it to be over. Maria agreed and also wanted to leave the celebration behind.

The bride and groom drove Walker's carriage, pulled by a big, beautiful, proud, white horse, and stopped at Hardy's home above the store, The Best Man would take care of the horse and buggy for the bride and groom.

***

As Hardy expected and wanted, he and Maria slept little during the night. Yet they woke on Sunday morning convinced they were the happiest people in town, maybe on planet Earth – if indeed they were *still on* planet Earth.

Neither could stop smiling.

The day before the wedding, Hardy attended to everything in his apartment. He cleaned the window, the stove, and the big washtub. He cleaned up the ashes and restocked the firewood. The Walkers gave him the day off on Saturday, his wedding day. Thinking ahead, he spent more than an hour at the local store and bought lots of groceries. He also bought breakfast biscuits at the café and stored them in the cupboard for Sunday morning. He wanted nothing to interfere with the new couple's first full day together.

He kissed Maria and gazed into her eyes. "Seems impossible, but I love you more than ever. So relax while I take care of breakfast."

182

Hardy eased out of bed and lit the firewood inside the stove. He dipped water from the bucket into the coffee pot, threw in two large scoops, and set the pot on the big iron burner.

Satisfaction filled Hardy's mind. *What more could a man need for happiness?*

Someone crept behind him and pinched him. "I need my new husband to hold me until breakfast is ready."

Hardy turned and pulled her close. "I need my hands to finish breakfast. And I need my new wife to hold me forever."

***

For dinner, Maria showed off her skills in the kitchen with a big meal, including dessert. Hardy expressed more than delight.

"Maria, you are full of surprises. I didn't know you could—"

Maria cocked her head. "You didn't know? You've had dinner at the Miller's place many times. And … when you were recovering from your head injury, I made most of your meals." She spread her hands and leaned toward him.

Hardy's forehead creased. "Are you telling me *you* are the one who …?"

"I've been Max and Nelda's housekeeper for over a year. Nelda taught me to cook. Just part of my job."

Hardy rose from the table, smiled into a small mirror on the wall. "How did you get so lucky, you big dummy?"

***

On their second night together, before they fell asleep, Hardy propped up on his elbows and stared down at the gorgeous lady on the pillow beside his, her face highlighted by the moonlight through the window.

183

She looked into his eyes. "Hardy, I like to believe we are together for a special reason, something far greater than just fate. *Think about it*. Two strangers from the same crazy world we barely remember. Yet we both ended up here, and each of us starts a new life. Then we meet, fall in love, get married and start another whole new life *together*."

A happy tear sparkled in the corner of her eye. "How could *anyone* top that?"

Hardy grinned. "I can't explain it, but I love it. And the longer I live here, the better it gets. I remember almost nothing about that old world, and that's the way I like it. I kept the same name but not much else."

"I understand, Hardy. I don't remember much either, but I didn't know what happiness was until I'd been here for a few months. Then, it seemed to grow and blossom. Now it's greater than I ever knew it could be."

Hardy grinned. "You told me you changed your name the day you got here. But you didn't tell me why."

"The name change was Seth's idea. Nelda suggested *Maria*, and Max said it goes well with *Miller*."

Hardy raised an eyebrow. "Seth was your agent?"

"Yes, Dear. I thought he was the only agent in Mystique."

Hardy shrugged. "Maybe so. I assumed we had more. So, do you remember your old name?"

Maria nodded.

"Nancy Naples."